Stan Davis began writing after retiring, drawing on his experience from a long and varied career.

Born in the Midlands, he worked as an apprentice toolmaker before completing his National Service as a clerk/storeman in the RAOC. He carried out stocktaking at an ammunition depot in Sherwood Forest.

He married a girl from the area and lives there today. He tried various jobs including butchery, grocery, and working in several timber yards.

Unsettled, he changed direction once more. He entered the world of selling. He was a sale representative for two companies for the final twenty-eight years of his working life.

He has a daughter and two grandchildren. His hobbies are gardening and cryptic crosswords.

Secrets of the Rio Negro

STAN DAVIS

Secrets of the
Rio Negro

Vanguard Press

A CIP catalogue record for this title is
available from the British Library.

ISBN: 978-1-84386-962-7

Vanguard Press is an imprint of
Pegasus Elliot Mackenzie Publishers Ltd.
www.pegasuspublishers.com

First Published in 2015
Vanguard Press

Sheraton House Castle Park
Cambridge England

Printed & Bound in Great Britain

Acknowledgements

Many thanks to Robert Judkins and the Production Department at Pegasus; with special thanks to Luke Irwin for accepting my complete manuscript for publication, and to proofreader Becky Stock.

Thanks too Carol and Roger for help with correspondence from Pegasus at various stages, and to Stuart Bell for his legal expertise.

To my family

Chapter 1

It was a grey, overcast November day. A cold Yorkshire mist found its way through my light clothes that had seemed adequate when I left Cornwall the previous day. Childhood memories were not the nostalgia I liked to rekindle and the reason I was here fuelled a slight air of misery. It only confirmed that I never expected a barrel of laughs. Living in the south most of my life I had become a southern softie. I had joined the north-south divide by association. It was a harsh condemnation of the county really and added to by sad memories of those early years. I was always prejudiced, I suppose, in retrospect. To visitors in the summer it was Brontë country with rolling moors and heather, bubbling brooks and country walks.

The reason I was here didn't help. Cemeteries the world over have a penchant for making visitors feel worse than they already do; this was no exception. Most of the headstones were blackened with age or edged with brown algae. The simple legend gave brief details of those beneath. Some of the words scarcely visible, as lichen and moss found sustenance in the crevices of the letters. My macabre sense of humour imagined the rows of decaying cadavers staring sightless at the lids of their tombs, with flesh no longer on their bones, wondering why their supposed loved ones had committed them to such a resting place. Most of those relatives, to my confirmed atheist mind, were only paying lip service to their various religious fears or dogma. They were afraid of what might befall them if they didn't conform to what was *proper*. I would prefer the ashes of a cremation when I am *aweary of this world*, as Shakespeare said.

Gradually the damp and the creatures that inhabited their surroundings would seek them out and devour what was edible. It was degradation, and a humiliation I hoped not to suffer. One or two of them, it's said, would turn in their graves due to some evilness of a misbehaving survivor and would be face down. Had a corpse from a re-opened coffin ever been discovered in that position, I wondered. If so, it would no doubt be blamed on a funeral director's assistant with necrophilic tendencies. I shivered as my mind ran off into an Edgar Allan Poe world. Evil visions of being molested after death spun round in my head. I mentally changed the subject and vowed that cremation would be a stipulation in my own last will and testament. I felt a slight sense of relief.

I stared at the newly engraved headstone of the particular one that I had eventually tracked down. There was a solitary spray of flowers already wilting in front of it. This was from some associate and would be a one-off. I placed my contribution next to it. A flower seller near the entrance had stirred my sense of guilt and I had fallen into the trap of conformity to which many had succumbed. I read the inscription.

William Henry Lockwood, b. Jan 10th 1935, d. Oct 15th 2000 it said briefly, but I knew that of course, I was his only son, Martin. It was black marble with gold lettering and pristine. At least it would stand the test of time. There was no additional couplet from a loved one, not even an RIP. Business-like and parsimonious as ever, it would have been all arranged years ago. It fulfilled its purpose. The scarcity of words sufficient, the expensive finish said it all. It reminded me of the flourish of his handwriting; he was confident in his ability. Its neighbours were similarly new. Subsequent rows gradually aged of course, until eventually they succumbed to the elements.

I had only spent my early years in the family home. We were always well off and I was never ill-treated. I simply can't recall any happy times. There must have been some but my brain had compressed them into dead files. There had been little father and son rapport except on rare occasions. No football kick-abouts in the garden, which was not surprising; he was more than forty years old when I entered his ordered life. My life-style was almost military. I conformed to the discipline that was never strict. It must have been boredom that dimmed my memory. I accepted it as the norm. It was a well-ordered and dull existence. Birthdays and Christmases I remember because of the costly presents that were never a let-down. I remember most of them even now. But I had no sibling to play with the trains and Meccano sets with me. I suppose I should have been more appreciative than I was. Later on, I was always luckier than most of my school friends in that respect. But it didn't seem that way when they described opening presents one by one with their parents, and the pranks, and laughter. I envied them.

I live in Cornwall now and haven't been back to Yorkshire since I left university. It was a sad homecoming and selfishly I wanted to return home as soon as I walked into the grey shadow of the house. Despite the weather and the misery of a deserted cemetery I didn't shed a tear or feel any regret for not having been closer to my father, although there was a sense of guilt for not being there when he died. We'd lived our lives separately and because I had no religious hang-ups, I didn't expect any retribution. My own conscience was more important to me. It is my God and my creed. That's why I never cheat at games – it's always watching.

My father, William Lockwood, had been a successful and highly competent solicitor and then barrister. The law and his involvement with it had occupied his waking thoughts throughout his life; at least that's what I had always thought and what he had once told me on a rare visit to Oxford and after a pleasant meal with a shared bottle of wine in a local restaurant. Later events were to explode that myth, but he was a lawyer and words were his tools, to be used to the best of his ability. A courtroom was a stage and the jury its audience. He was Olivier and hoped his performance would earn their plaudits and condemn his opponent. Star billing meant suitable rewards to enhance his life-style.

He had concentrated on being the best in his field and he wanted me to follow in his footsteps. I'm afraid his words fell on stony ground and this had hardened with the distance that separated us. I hadn't inherited his nose-to-the-grindstone application. There had never been an urgency to do well as he had deemed necessary. The stuffy atmosphere of the courtroom with its wigs and gowns never appealed to me. Despite his coaxing I knew I would choose something with less of the restrictions that ruled in the confines and legalities of his world.

The first female that changed his dedication to success in business was a young female doctor from the local hospital. He successfully defended her in a malpractice suit. It was a complicated case and the hospital had thrust the onus of responsibility on to her and dismissed her at the same time. She was therefore forced to defend herself and could ill afford to. Their big guns were brought into play to avoid a possible huge compensation. She was young and beautiful and he fell for her charms. He took on the case pro bono and was suitably rewarded both financially and career-wise, it turned out. Even students at Oxford studying law had heard about him. Afterwards, inexperienced as he was to female wiles, the whole thing went to his head or some other part of his anatomy and he proposed.

They married quickly and she became pregnant almost at once, much to his annoyance. He hadn't really thought of the radical change on his staid social life, written in stone. I came to this conclusion years later. There is little gratification in hindsight, he learned to his cost. As I matured and experienced sex and the female psyche, I got the picture. He may have won the battle in the courtroom, but she had won the war and achieved her real goal. It would be unlikely that any other hospital would employ her after her success in the trial. She had a fairly good settlement from them and would see my father as a good prospect for an easy life from there on. She could now reap the benefit. On the other hand, my father never appeared a barrel of laughs or a party animal. Perhaps I misjudged her, I shall never know.

I was the result of this seduction and quickly became aware of their incompatibility even as a young boy; there were constant rows. Maybe it was a sexual problem because of their age difference. I was too young to even know about such things. I do know she spent most of her time reading books and magazines. She attended to all my needs but little else, apart from a cuddle now and then. Meals were rarely on time and mostly from the freezer. The house would be untidy when my father came home even though it was late. He would rail her about these things. She would say he stayed late drinking with his pals and so the evenings were passed in silence and I was ignored. His orderly lifestyle was turned upside down.

They were oblivious to my feelings as their bitterness grew, and I was the bone of their contention it appeared to me. Even at that tender age I felt responsible for their unhappiness. It couldn't go on, and didn't.

Things came to a head, and she left him and disappeared with a young doctor. I have wondered since how she came to meet him. I know I was young but I have no recollection of ever having seen her with any other man, not at home or when we were out.

On the day she went I had no intimation. In the afternoon, she came downstairs with a suitcase packed. I asked where we were going and she said nowhere. She said very little to me and read a book silently. Looking back, she appeared sad and fidgety at the same time. As my father came into the living room, she picked up the suitcase and marched past him and out of the front door without a word. It was one of the few occasions that I saw him actually agitated. He stood there non-plussed for some time. I stared at him. I had no idea what was going on. I'm sure it was a face he had never displayed in court. I believe a waiting car picked her up, probably her lover. Eventually my father pulled himself together and I watched him pour a large whisky and sit on the settee. He patted the seat beside him for me to join him. He drank a good measure from his glass and when he was more composed, mumbled a reason for my mother's disappearance. It was off the top of his head and not worthy of a courtroom. I was only three or four and have no idea what he said, or what it meant.

We never heard from her again. I have never lost the image of that day. It's the only one that I remember from my childhood.

For the first few weeks after she left, my father stayed at home to look after me and neglected his practice. I had all his attention and he coped very well, but then he'd always been efficient in everything he did. I had all his attention and the only really happy times I remember with him. After the initial trauma he seemed happier too. Perhaps he enjoyed this new father and son relationship that had been thrust on him. Perhaps he had learned a lesson that there was much more to life than the courtroom.

Whatever it was, it didn't last long and numerous phone calls and visits from fellow barristers wore him down. Once more he threw himself into his briefs, to coin a phrase. He engaged a full-time nanny-housekeeper and gradually he retreated into his legal war of words. He did however, find a little time for me at the weekends. Even then he was wrapped up in his work and endeavouring to sort through papers at the same time. As before, I engaged his attention less and less. I learned at Oxford that he was one of the top barristers and his fees were enormous. I certainly reaped the benefits from his earnings, so I shouldn't have any complaints.

I think I was about five or maybe older when he packed me off to a boarding school. In those few short years, I had experienced the happiness of a small child, followed by the increasing bitterness of the arguments. I lost whom I thought was a loving mother and finally, I seemed to have been rejected or at least ignored by my father. In my adult years I decided I had been the scapegoat and not the reason. They were the guilty ones. I quickly removed that chip from my shoulder.

Most of the other boys at boarding school were of similar backgrounds and I regarded my new life as normal. This is what happened to boys from middle class families, I thought. We were sent there to be brought up in an ordered and disciplined way. I felt no resentment towards my father for being there and I was well treated. It was a good school and I enjoyed my time there. I never wanted for anything and a phone-call home was all that was necessary to not feel deserted. I was one of the luckier ones.

Through those early years, I only saw my father during school holidays and occasionally when he would pop over for a weekend. He usually brought a gift or had tickets for events. Nothing was too much trouble for him. Churlishly I suppose I put it down to his guilty conscience. It never appeared to be a chore to him and now I think he enjoyed those weekends with me, but we were never close. On one or two occasions someone at school mistook him for my grandfather. I had once seen him rehearsing a closing speech in front of a mirror at home; the white wig only emphasised his age. He gripped one side of his gown and pointed a finger at an imaginary defendant. It was quite theatrical.

When I grew older he would sometimes pat me on the back and shake my hand if I excelled in my studies. I never got a hug. It was the sort of thing I imagined he did with colleagues and opponents alike after court cases. Those battles left him with little time for sentiment so I excused him. The visits became more rare as I grew older and taller and the congratulations appeared stilted and condescending, finally disappearing altogether. I progressed through my various schools with very little trouble academically. He never received bad reports from tutors and he was more than pleased when I obtained a place at Oxford. He suggested I take driving lessons, gave me a cheque to cover six lessons and when I finally passed, a second-hand MG sports car was delivered from a local dealer. A letter from him said it was a reward for my academic achievements. It was quite formal as if I were a godson, which was only to be expected. He was never going to break the habit of a lifetime.

I settled into digs at Oxford and it was a happy part of my life; that much I do know. I'd finally shed any angst from memories of my younger days and became one of a community of young men and women, most of them striving earnestly towards a degree. It was refreshing and I felt really grown up. A cheque arrived on the first of every month and it was very generous. Unlike some of the students I didn't need to worry about money and find part-time work. The MG life added icing on the cake and my future at the university became assured. My childhood anxieties and hang-ups were a thing of the past.

My father never came down while I was at university at all. I suppose it showed his trust in me. We corresponded by letter; his were typed and no doubt dictated to his secretary. Eventually I did realise how lucky I was. I'd heard it enough times from the other students during my years there. I knuckled down to my studies, determined to do well. I may not have wanted to practice law but I vowed to get good grades.

I would telephone him if I needed anything urgently, or maybe tickets that were hard to come by for some event; he always seemed to come up trumps. I took it for granted that he knew the right people. Our conversations were friendly but never warm. He was more like that kindly rich godfather I suppose most of my friends assumed he was.

Certain memories raced through my mind as I stood staring at the gold lettering. It had been a strange relationship for father and son, especially as there was no real animosity between us. I reproached myself for not making an effort to thank him properly for his generosity towards me. But it was reciprocal I suppose; he'd never given me a normal home life. I ungraciously apportioned the blame.

I knew I could never return to live with him after university. There were no happy childhood memories that my fellow students were constantly recounting to me when they returned from term breaks. It would be almost like settling in to live with an uncle. He was after all, forty years older than me. We wouldn't have hit it off and would end up as enemies. As it was, he would die satisfied I had received a good education. I had the consolation that he would never have to turn in his grave.

The house was on the outskirts of Ripon and I only remembered that it had always looked bleak and forbidding. The memories of my parents arguing were a constant reminder during my time at Oxford and helped to keep us at arm's length. At the same time I never tried to contact my mother and that too was mutual. I knew very little about her and we would have nothing in common. The whole thing was frustrating and the feeling of unease never left me. I never exorcised it. I would recall lying in bed, listening to the two of them and trying to understand some of the adult implications. But I was too young to understand about sex, so I never apportioned blame. Individually they both loved me; I just wanted them to be the loving parents that I'd read about in books and seen in films. It probably influenced my own behaviour and consequentially I never had close friends, male or female, as I grew up. Compared to them I was spoiled financially and a future career never clouded my horizon as theirs did. They were always thinking of their plans after university: what sort of career would they have? Who would they marry? I envied most of them as they described their weekends at home with their families. I compensated by getting the most out of my own little world at weekends. Girlfriends were never a problem as I always had the wherewithal to take them out, but I never became serious with a particular one. I was determined not to get involved or make commitments. I was completely selfish. In retrospect, I was a sad case really, disillusioned before adulthood. My excuse was the example that I had witnessed.

The MG became my alter ego. It was the other half to a life of pleasure and the envy of some of my fellow students. I was never short of a girlfriend in my free time. My mind was blotting paper for facts and figures, and while my fellow students were swatting up at the weekend I would be inviting some girl or other to go for a spin, usually adding to my sex education, but not always of course. I didn't set out to seduce them and there was no pressure. If I struck up a friendship with a girl in the cafeteria or one of the Bodleian libraries, I'd take her out a couple of times just for the pleasure of having dinner with a pretty girl. If she lived a reasonable distance from the university, I'd offer to drive her home at the weekend or on a mid-term break. I'd just enjoy her company and see where it went.

One of these outings was to Cornwall where this particular girl lived. Her name was Julie and we really did bump into each other. It was in the Ashmolean Museum. I was idling my time at the weekend with nothing planned and eventually wandered round to one of the art sections. There was an exhibition of modern artists and I was trying to make out which way up a particular art palette of garish colours was and tilted my head to the right. She was doing likewise from the left and we collided. We laughed and agreed immediately about the merits of the artwork: zero. We went for a coffee to get the taste out of our mouths. We laughed quite a lot on our first meeting and we went out a couple of times. She insisted on going Dutch and that was fine by me because she seemed a very independent sort and I liked that. She was pretty and not too hung up on studies, so we didn't talk shop. That was a change. I offered to drive her home for the mid-term break and she said I could sleep in the spare room for my generosity. She was so casual and laid back about it all, as if we were two lads. She's one that stuck in my mind over the years because the weather was fine and so was the sex. That's why I remember her name. There was almost inevitability about our friendship, we had the same attitude towards life. She was a free spirit with a good allowance like me, so there was no penny-pinching on dates by either of us. From the start I could tell we would end up in bed even though there were no innuendos by either of us. Her parents were also divorced and she lived with her mother. Her father was a stockbroker in the City so she and her mother were well provided for. I think she inherited this liberal attitude towards sex from her mother, hence the divorce I guess. She let Julie have free rein and there was no worry about me staying there, she laughed. Her present boyfriend – the mother's that is – was an actor of very little reputation. A much younger man but handsome of course, a toy-boy.

Julie and I saw little of them during that week. Her mother had gone up to London and stayed in a hotel to be near her latest as he acted out a minor role in the theatre. This left the house for us to come and go as we liked. Sexually we had a great time without the usual hole-in-the-wall subterfuge that's normally associated with youthful liaisons. Julie wasn't worried about commitments and I took advantage of it. During the day we would drive around the beautiful Cornish countryside, calling at village pubs for lunch and evening meals and then making love. It was paradise for both of us, and unreal. Certainly not what I'd experienced before with college girls. As the week wore on I felt I was falling in love with her and marriage would be inevitable, yet it was not what I had in mind at this time.

I must have read too much into it because after the romance of that holiday week, things cooled down very quickly when we returned to college. I'd see her in one of the libraries or some other place of study; we'd chat and have a coffee and arrange a date. I was at Balliol, she at St Anne's or St Hilda's; I can't remember which now as there were other girls during those years. Julie and I would usually go to a local cinema and a restaurant after. I'd suggest a night in a hotel, as my car was too small for comfortable sex. I found out early on that there's nothing more off-putting for a girl than the end of a gear stick poking her in the thigh.

She didn't seem keen, saying it sounded sordid and it was too close to the university, as if she didn't want to be seen by a fellow student. I took her to London one weekend and we went to a show. I suggested staying the night but she made an excuse about her period. I knew then that it had gone sour. A few weeks later she had another boyfriend in tow. He had an athletic figure and was destined to be an Olympic swimmer in the future: I paled in comparison. I had been a handy chauffeur, I reflected. He also had a newer car and was from an aristocratic background. There were no hard feelings on either side. She had added to my sex education in no small way and I breathed a sigh of relief that in the long term there had been no commitments. I had learned another lesson. I may have had a car and not been short of money, but I wasn't the bee's knees. After that, I vowed to keep the relationships short.

The memory that really stuck in my mind from that episode was our visit to the Eden Project when we were in Cornwall.

It had only been open a couple of years and, as biochemistry was one of my subjects, it fascinated me. There were whole ecosystems being developed under giant transparent domes and I was hooked. Why not? I thought. It was a possible career that I could enjoy. If I got my degree it would help. So I applied for a position there after university. It was six months before they accepted me. During the interim, I remained in my digs in Oxford and even dated a few of the girls that were on offer, some of them one-night stands. Some of them I'd like to forget.

I telephoned my dad about Eden and my enthusiasm was enough to convince him that I'd never follow in his footsteps. He raised no objections; in fact he seemed pleased that at least I was contemplating getting a job, and if I enjoyed it, so much the better. My polite enquiries as to how business was going got their usual "splendid". He told me not to rush into anything and added that he was increasing my allowance. The conversation didn't go much beyond that.

True to his word, my generous monthly cheques continued to arrive. With time on my hands and a fairly decent summer, I took advantage of it. I drove to various resorts in the south. Bournemouth was the most enjoyable of these and the sun was particularly hot. I stayed a week and swam and lazed on the beach during the days. At night the pubs were full. Most of the young people sat outside in the cooler air. I joined in conversations but all the girls were either with their boyfriends or part of a hen night. There was little chance of me scoring. Still, it blew the cobwebs out of my academically stuffed brain cells.

Finally came the letter for a start date at the Eden Project. I drove down to fix up somewhere to live and the nearest town was St Austell. I found the tourist office and, although they tried, there was no accommodation available on a regular basis. It was the height of summer and to be expected. I was given a few addresses in the surrounding area and finally got fixed up in the outskirts of Charelstown. It was only a few miles from the Eden Project and an attic flat. The price didn't make much of a dent in my budget and it was clean. There was a small kitchen/dining area and the double bedroom clinched it for me. On a clear day I would have a sea view. It was an ideal spot.

Up to that point in my life I had been pretty well featherbedded. I appreciated once more how lucky I was. Without too much effort I'd got through university and not missed out on the finer things in life. I was young, fairly fit and felt confident of my future. I was quickly brought down to earth at the Eden Project. I was now an employee among the lower echelon and a day's work was expected for the salary, which was not a large amount but extra to my allowance, and there was no reduction in that. There were physical demands I'd never experienced at Oxford; even so I enjoyed it. My first job was amongst the tropical plants. The atmosphere was humid and a shower was always something to look forward to at the end of each day. It was the first inkling I had of my father's interests as a young man. Something he'd never spoke about. I thought it was only right to tell him how the job was going and thank him for my increased allowance, so I phoned him.

He brushed aside my thanks and seemed genuinely interested to hear about the effects of the microclimate in the biospheres. He obviously had read all about them, but then he would do, he never did things by halves. That was why he was a successful barrister. He hung on my every word and for the first time in my life I enjoyed our conversation. It was the tip of an iceberg that only fully emerged much later.

He began to phone me on a more regular basis and asked me questions as if he was really interested, unlike our conversations while I was at Oxford. As I enthused about the wonders of the tropical forests and the various plants that I was attending to, he would make some casual remark. At first I thought he was being patronising to his only offspring, but now I realise his comments were tongue-in-cheek. He really knew about these things but didn't let on. In my youthful exuberance I never picked up on it. Because of his general aloofness that was part of his makeup and his calling, I never suspected that he knew more than I did about the subject. He never enlightened me as he could have done. As I reached this point in my memory I turned away from the black slab of marble, frustrated. Things could have been so different if he hadn't been consumed with success as a barrister and I had not been concerned only with the selfishness of youth. I left the cemetery and hoped these confused thoughts would stay with the dead. I was still dwelling on the past as I drove up the drive to the old grey-stoned house where I had spent my childhood. I knew I would have to spend at least one night here.

Chapter 2

I had a meeting there with the local solicitor. It was he who had written to tell me of the death of my father from a heart attack and to inform me of arrangements for the funeral. The letter had arrived the day after I had left for a holiday in Majorca. With my usual carefree attitude I couldn't be traced and missed the funeral, adding to the guilt in my conscience. I had telephoned the solicitor's office the day before and had arranged to meet him at the house at three o'clock. It was five minutes to the hour as I drove up. At least I wasn't late. He would no doubt view me as some prodigal son turning up for his inheritance to fritter it away. When we spoke on the phone he intimated that the meeting would be about the will. My mother had remarried so I was the sole beneficiary; that much I knew. Money, or the shortage of it had never clouded my horizon. I couldn't imagine I would be worse off after my appointed meeting. I hoped that the sun would shine on my finances even more after today.

I felt a slight feeling of excitement as Joseph Wilmott opened the door to me, but tried not to show it. The need for money had never been in the forefront of my mind and maybe

I acted slightly more blasé about the whole thing than he expected.

Nevertheless he was very friendly and we warmed to each other quickly. He asked me to call him Joseph; it was what my father did.

During our conversation it became obvious that my father had known him for years and had been quite proud of my academic endeavours. Joseph Wilmott was a tall but slight figure with a stoop. This was caused by years of poring over legal papers at a desk that was too low, or a seat that was too high. At least that's what my twisted sense of humour came up with. Not for him the cut and thrust of the courtroom as my father. His exercise was confined to reaching and lifting down a legal book from the shelves around his office. He passed on difficult cases too and they became a brief for my father. In turn he did a lot of spadework for him. He enjoyed the mundane paper work of house sales, probates and the occasional divorce settlements. His only vice it seemed, was an old Bristol car. I admired its singularity for a few minutes before ringing the bell. Although he had tended it carefully, it was beginning to show its age.

He quickly broke down the barrier between solicitor and client with the usual pleasantries. His own son was at Cambridge and he politely asked for my view on the Oxbridge scene. His questions were pertinent without being personal and he seemed genuinely interested and not condescending. It was an attitude he had perfected over the years. Clients would open up to him easily with their personal feelings. Finally he got down to the reason for our meeting.

'I arranged our first meeting here,' he said, 'so that I could give you the keys to the property and you could stay here till the will is finally probated, if you wish, or at least look around before you return home.' It was pretty obvious that over the years my father had kept him up to date with my progress and Joseph had a reasonably good opinion of me. He was also aware of why I lived away. He pointed to a cardboard box on the table.

'There are some groceries in the box. Milk and other fresh foods are in the fridge. They will last you for at least a few days.' I could see why my father had retained his services over the years. I thanked him.

'In the event that you may wish to live here, Martin.' His glance told me he knew the answer to that. 'If not, then during your stay here you may wish to look around and select personal items of your father's that you may want to keep. As executor to your father's will, I have no objection to that; there are no other relatives involved, the contents are all yours if you wish.

'I will read out the brief terms today. I would like you to come to my office on Monday to go over it in detail and sign the usual papers of acceptance. Mr Lockwood intimated that you may want to sell the property and there is a codicil to that effect. If for any reason you wish to contract the sale yourself I would have no objection. I would point out that your father trusted us with these type of transactions in the past and we have local contacts.' I said I had no objections and he seemed pleased that I accepted his honesty without question. He outlined the bare bones of the will.

The first page was all about my father's business and how that was to be settled. All departments had been seamlessly transferred before his death to colleagues and junior partners. It was all neat and tidy and at the end of it, the solicitor asked if I'd any objections to any part of it. I shook my head with a wry smile. It was all above my head and he knew, so he continued with the rest, which was simple.

Apart from the house and after the usual deductions for tax, solicitor's fees and outstanding debts, I would eventually receive about £265,000. It was a huge sum and I gulped, but managed to display no signs of my elation visibly. It was far more than I'd expected. My father had lived life to the full. He had a Rolls Bentley, ate in the best restaurants and drank the best wines and whiskies. The latter had probably contributed to the heart attack that had taken him. But he was a good barrister and an expensive one. His success rate ensured that his charges and expenses always floated upwards. Mr Wilmott seemed suitably impressed with my aplomb.

'I have no intention of living here, as you may have guessed,' I told him immediately, 'so I would be grateful if you will supervise the sale of the house for me, Joseph, as I shall be returning to Cornwall as soon as possible. However, I shall spend a few days here first in case there are any mementoes I may want to take with me. I can tell from our conversation that you and he had a rapport from years of honest dealings with each other. I trust you implicitly as I'm sure he did. In spite of the fact that this is our first meeting, I sense that you know as much about me as he did.' I paused and he smiled.

'You seem to have inherited some of his astuteness in dealing with people too, Martin. And charm,' he added. *Touché*, I thought.

'There's a painting or two and one or two small pieces of furniture that I've heard my father mention that were dear to him. I think he would purchase one after a particularly rewarding victory. He'd tell me about it and I would see if it was worth a mention in the Ashmolean. When I've decided which ones I prefer, perhaps you could arrange to have them sent down to my home address. I won't risk taking them in my MG. As for the rest, perhaps you could contact some local auction house to dispose of them. The proceeds could go to some worthy cause of your choice, Joseph, with a mention of where they came from. Maybe a local charity shop could pick up his clothes after I've sorted through them. None of them would fit me anyway but there may be cufflinks and other accessories I could keep for keepsakes. Certainly not for sentimental reasons, it's not one of my finer senses. I'll go through his personal papers and photographs too. I'll keep any I think fit and burn the rest on the fire in the living room. I think that's all unless there is anything I've missed. I'll see you on Monday, perhaps you can look in your diary now and give me a time.'

'What about the Bentley?' he said rather quickly, and I detected a hidden agenda in his voice.

'Why, where you interested in it yourself?' I answered, innocently enough. He smiled weakly.

'Well, yes actually.'

'Then it's yours at bottom book price,' I said in the manner of Arthur Daley or some other used car salesman. 'Less ten percent commission for your good self,' I continued in the same vein. 'Is that a fair deal, Guv?' His face broke into a smile.

'Indeed, Martin, that will do nicely,' and he fairly beamed. There was no way I could drive to the Eden project in a Bentley and it didn't compete with my MG for attracting the girls, although it would have been more comfortable for sex on the back seat. He gave me a time for my Monday appointment. Before he drove away I saw him glance towards the garage where the Bentley was housed and sensed his elation. He would have admired it longingly many times in the past. I'm sure it was going to a good home.

Chapter 3

By the time he left the sun had gone down and I shivered. I went outside and in the garage I found firelighters and sticks. Outside the back door I'd seen the pile of logs stacked up and carried a sufficient of them in a wickerwork basket on hand for the purpose. It was satisfying to carefully set about lighting the fire in the huge grate. While it was burning up, I made a coffee and poured a large brandy from the decanter into a crystal goblet from the display case. I gazed at the sets of expensive glasses that would be torn from their imperious surroundings. I promised to take a select few with me to impress someone in my own circle.

I pulled the oak coffee table closer to the fire, regardless of any possible heat damage it would suffer. I had spent little time here since my childhood but not much had changed in the large living room. Most of my young life had been spent in rented rooms. Owning property had never come into the equation. At that moment, despite not wanting to stay here, I suddenly felt Lord of the Manor. All this was mine: the roaring fire, the expensive bottles of spirits and the crystal glasses. I sat for some time daydreaming about the future now that I was financially secure. I drained the brandy glass and twirled it between cupped hands slowly between each sip as I had observed my father do. The fire was now showing its worth and I circumspectly showed a little more respect for the table by moving it away. The heat from the burning logs and the brandy were soothing and I poured another generous measure from the crystal decanter. I imagined my father doing exactly the same in his loneliness and maybe thinking of me. I reproached myself mentally for scarcely ever doing the same whilst at Oxford, thinking of him that is. But recriminations were pointless now and my selfishness dismissed the thoughts. Yet they lingered on what could have been. This huge house so tastefully furnished, with no thought of cost, had never been a happy home. I hoped it would be in the future.

I went from room to room with a certain thrill of anticipation, wondering what I would discover. The house had acquired that mustiness I had observed initially, throughout. All the services were still laid on, I'd been told by Joseph, and I found the cupboard containing the central heating. Although ancient-looking, it responded to my manipulations as per the instructions from Mr Wilmott. It had been serviced meticulously. There was a large radiator in each room and it was my intention to make sure the property lost its smell of neglect before I left. Nevertheless, it was still clean and tidy due to the diligence of cleaners hired by Joseph. By the time I eventually departed I would lose some of my initial misgivings of the place. Many years of bad memories had stoked those ill-feelings. My childhood memories were responsible for those.

I made a note of items I intended to have delivered to Cornwall. The oak coffee table was high on the list, for obvious reasons. It had seemed to welcome me as I sat by the fire. The only other piece of furniture that took my eye was the Welsh dresser. It was filled with all the pottery necessary for mealtimes. I'm sure I could find room for it in my flat, perhaps get it cut down. Some of the pieces in it had survived from the days of my mother. I must have that and certain items that I remember from my childhood. Apart from the squabbles, I think she loved me. I know she spoilt me. Nostalgia started to make me greedy for the past; I must stop.

Even with my scant knowledge of art, I could see there were several valuable paintings amongst the numerous ones in all the rooms. I would take some of the smaller ones with me when I left. I'd find room for a couple of the best and sell the rest through an art gallery.

My father had never owned a computer. His own financial affairs would have been taken care of by the man who had just left along with various accountants. He had a competent secretary in his office who saw to all the paperwork involved and left him to concentrate on his court appearances. I discovered from Joseph Wilmott that he had wound down the business during the last few years for health reasons. In the event of his death, Mrs Wilson, the secretary, would be taken care of and cases on hand at that time would be handed over to capable associates. In his usual efficient way my father had left no loose ends. Of course, he had never let on to me about his health problems. It was another prick to my conscience and something I would have to come to terms with.

Living on his own and with his clinical mind there was very little personal stuff that needed burning. He'd even got rid of most of the family photographs since my mother's departure.

He would have anticipated his demise at some point and, living alone, would have made sure there were no skeletons to be unearthed. I did find a slim album of their honeymoon photographs. He'd probably cherished it as the only happiness he'd got out of the marriage. The pictures were taken on a Greek island, going by the inscriptions on the tavernas. Happiness shone from all of the images. My mother had a beautiful figure and my father too was tanned, even though his hair was beginning to recede at the front. He was still slim. Perhaps he'd made an effort to capture my mother. They were good photographs; I think photography was one of his hobbies. I can't remember the pair of them looking so happy as a child. It was the culmination of a brief courtship and then I spoiled it all, or so I always believed. Perhaps there was more to it than that.

Even now, after a university education and reading all the classics, I am still trying to understand the difference between love and sex. There are so many nuances.

'Nuances can be nuisances,' I mused out loud.

I was in the bathroom and it echoed back to me. It wasn't as funny as I thought. At college I would have expected at least a titter from someone and a groan from the rest as I came out with one of my puns. The ten-year-old brandy was having an effect. I decided it was time for bed.

Without thinking, I went to my old bedroom. It was empty and I was glad. I don't think I could have slept easy there. I went along to the master bedroom and gazed around. It looked exactly as I remembered it all those years ago. The double bed had been stripped, of course. I opened the blanket box and it was full of clean linen. I slowly made up the bed, looking at the furnishings as I did so; very little had changed. I went to the bathroom, stripped down to my boxers and climbed into bed. There was an alarm-clock-radio on a shelf in the headboard. I fiddled with it and found some late night music station. The cotton sheets were cool but comfortable and I went over the events of the day. I knew sleep wouldn't come easy: an unfamiliar bed and all that had happened. But it wasn't just that. Unlike my flat, the house was huge. I imagined I was back there as a boy, a small boy in a big bed with no one to cuddle me.

Despite my mental histrionics at bedtime, I slept soundly and couldn't wait to explore all the rooms in the hope of finding ghosts in the closets. Joseph had excelled with the provisions and I could have had a cooked breakfast but I was too eager to delve. I had orange juice, toast and tea. I resisted the brandy till mid-morning and had a small one with coffee.

I was hoping to find some letters from a secret lover or some other family scandal unknown to me. Fiction writers have a lot to answer for. Nevertheless, I was perhaps a little disappointed but at the same time relieved when none came to light.

I started in the bedroom and worked my way down. I emptied the contents of the built-in wardrobe onto the bed for collection by a charity shop. Most of the clothes were sombre suits suitable for his profession or Rotary Club occasions. Most of the shirts and shoes were in keeping with his lifestyle. The evening suit was immaculate and had nothing in the pockets except an expensive cigar in a leather case, of course. There were a few casual items for when he sat in the garden in the summer months. Along the bottom were his current camera and a briefcase. There were a number of old cameras that he'd been loath to part, with as hobbyists do; as another of advanced specification superseded the previous one. His aim for perfection made him a good customer. The most expensive was a Leica. I intended taking them all back with me. It seemed sacrilege to let them go to a charity shop. As I brought the briefcase into the light I recognised it and it stirred memories. I'd forgotten all about it over the years but remembered the very smell of it. Nostalgia stopped me in my tracks as I rolled back the years till the night I last saw it.

It had been a rare occasion not long after my mother had deserted us. Now and then my father would go to a dinner or some other social do with the Rotary, the Conservative and so many others clubs that were pleased to enrol him. The members and their wives weren't the sort of people my mother took to. She was from a working class background and, to her credit, excelled at school. She remained a staunch Socialist despite her new circle of friends and much to my father's annoyance. They usually returned home in silence or arguing politics. It was another sticking point in their relationship, perhaps the main reason for the end of the marriage. Very soon she refused to go with him. *A small pearl of wisdom etched itself into the subconscious of Martin Lockwood. When choosing a future spouse, make sure that you are both compatible in mind as well as flesh.* He continued to go without her and shortly afterwards she left. Perhaps the politics were a side issue and the break-up was inevitable. He was distraught, probably because it disrupted his well-ordered life and soon engaged a full-time live-in housekeeper. She had her own room.

She doubled as a sitter for me on the one or two evenings he went to his clubs. At other times it would be a young relative of hers. They would be taken home by taxi.

It was on such an occasion that I first saw the briefcase. He usually had his fair share of whiskies on these occasions and on this particular night was in a mellow mood. I'd had a nightmare and Mrs Hadley, the housekeeper, was the sitter. She was trying to calm me down when he arrived.

He said she could toddle off to bed and he'd let me stay up with him for a while till I'd calmed down. I'd seen him drunk before and heard my mother getting on to him about it. Because of the alcohol he had lost some of the normal legal coldness that I was used to. He seemed more loving than I had ever seen him before. He sat me on his knee and became sad-faced as he stared into the embers of the fire. Tears welled up in his eyes and he murmured my mother's name. I put my arms round him because he looked so sad. He became a little maudlin I suppose, looking back. I asked him to read me a story as my mother did sometimes. He had no stories of course, so he fetched this leather case from his study. I opened it now and the memories flooded back.

His parents were quite well off and, like me, he never wanted for anything. It was the first time he'd confided in me about anything. He spoke to me as if I were an adult – the whisky I suppose. He was confiding in me. He probably regretted doing so the next day and he never mentioned it again.

I do remember that faraway look, as if I wasn't there, as he related those early years. I dare say he'd probably never opened his heart to another person about the details before. Perhaps

42

my mother, but I doubt it. I think their relationship was romance and sunny holidays followed by bitterness.

As I recall, he said he had no trouble getting his law degree. It was a statement of fact I remember, not bragging. He slurred his words and they were so quiet I could barely hear them. He was single-minded and pragmatic; nothing distracted him from his goal. That is my interpretation now of what he said then. He'd studied hard and after university his parents suggested taking some time off before joining his first law firm as a junior, a kind of reward for his academic achievement. It was exactly as he did for me; he too had not been pressed to find a job.

More of it came back to me now. I think he'd forgotten I was on his lap and spoke as if he were addressing a jury, telling them the facts. Most of it was too grown up for me. I wanted a bedtime story and he had none.

He took a year off he said; a sabbatical I suppose it would be. He then described his journey around South America after he left England for that year. First of all he travelled along the Amazon. That's all I remember, I must have fallen asleep before he'd finished his travelogue. He evidently put me to bed and then went to the bathroom to get ready for bed himself. He returned and peeped in to see if I was OK. The creak of the door must have stirred me. I could only see his bare trunk as he leaned in, and noticed a large scar on the inside of his upper right arm, just above his elbow. My bedside nightlight illuminated it clearly; it looked purple. He always wore long-sleeved shirts even in the summer and that explained it. I asked him about it a few days later when the memory surfaced and he dismissed my question in his usual offhand manner. He said it was a scar from some operation or other.

I asked him to tell me more about his adventures as I hadn't heard the end, but he never did. It was as if he was embarrassed about disclosing as much as he had. What he did say had virtually faded until I saw the case. Now it all came back and I was intrigued.

I gazed once more at the contents. Mostly it was photographs he'd taken himself with that old but expensive Leica, the one in the bottom of the wardrobe still in its leather case. I looked at them now with more interest. Some of them I hadn't seen because I'd fallen asleep. They were black and white and taken in the jungle somewhere. I had to stare at them to recognise that the photos were of him. They must have been taken when he had graduated and taken a year off. I began to put two and two together.

With the knowledge I'd gained in my present employment I became excited to see plants in their true environment. I remembered how I'd told him about the amazing collection at the Eden Project in my phone-calls and letters. I felt a little deflated seeing those photos of the real thing and imagining him being there in their true habitat. He had known more about them than I did and never let on. The black and white pictures didn't give them justice of course. I could just imagine how the flora and fauna would look with a modern camera. Yet here was evidence of all he had seen during his time in Manaus and the surrounding rainforests; for that's where his journey had started. There were notes on the back of some of the photographs to remind him where they were taken. There were only a few photos of my father, probably taken by some of the natives after tuition from him. These local natives were in evidence in the rest of the collection of snapshots. They wore very few clothes and the girls were topless. One of them stood next to him and he looked slightly embarrassed, but struck a theatrical pose for the benefit of the camera. Most of my memories of him were in clerical, grey suits and I could scarcely imagine him surrounded by these wild people posing in such a manner. With his pith helmet and long, khaki shorts he was the epitome of the old jungle explorer, although he looked a little more Eric Morecambe than Stanley or Livingstone. It was doubtful if any members of his various clubs would recognise him without his pinstripes and wig. One of them was taken in the shade and he had removed his helmet. I only remember a receding hairline but here it was much thicker. With a thin, pencil moustache that was the vogue at the time he had the looks of Douglas Fairbanks Junior and with his slim figure, quite handsome. There were over a hundred photographs in all. I remember my phone-calls and the way I had gone on about the Eden Project. He must have smiled to himself. I can't remember him showing me any of this collection. Perhaps he did and I fell asleep before he made his appearance in any of them.

I know I fell asleep and don't even remember him carrying me to bed. I certainly didn't recall them when I told him about my job at the Eden Project. He just let me carry on as I enthused about my job and there was no put-down remark at the end. I wish he had mentioned them.

Also in the briefcase was a waterproof folder, musty and slightly mildewed. He would have carried this around with him during his expedition. In it were notebooks obviously scribbled at the time. Already I began to get the feeling of the conditions he was exposed to during his time in the Brazilian rainforest. The humidity was obvious from the condition of the paper. I was working in a similar environment at the Eden Project but my father had experienced the added dangers of diseases, deadly creatures, intense heat, tropical rains and countless other perils. Things I'd only read about. My place of work was a paradise compared to what he'd endured. I dearly wished I had known about all this years ago. I would certainly have held him in awe. I'm sure our brief meetings at Oxford would have been more enjoyable had he told me about all this. What he'd seen was something else, to put it mildly. Even the monochrome images didn't convey the intensity of the heat and humidity. I spent over an hour studying the photographs and the notebooks. They were worlds apart from the bewigged barrister that I knew. At a stroke the slightly portly urbane figure of the law courts became an intrepid adventurer and explorer. Clark Kent had become Superman; I envied him for what I saw before me.

The only other item in the briefcase was a penknife, and what a penknife. It was a Swiss Army knife and, because of where I'd found it, must have been something special he had bought for his expedition. It was in pristine condition and obviously had been kept so. Here was the odour of good quality machine oil, and the individual implements still displayed in an arc at each end at the touch of a finger and thumbnail with ease. There was a loop to attach it to a belt at the waist. It was Swiss of course and cost three pounds fifteen shillings, including postage. The receipt was in the case to prove it. At the time it would be half a week's wages for a working man. It had a white, dimpled, bone handle and was a work of art. He must have carried it with him on that journey. He was alone in Brazil and it was a friend of some quality, to remind him of the good things that he admired, like brandy and a Cuban cigar. It had a knife, fork and spoon, plus many other implements for every possible emergency. If the worst came to the worst it was a weapon. Pride of place in his equipment would be that Swiss knife. I snapped the knife into its ready position. I could see it had been kept honed to a razor's edge by my father on his travels. Sharpening it on any stone that was available. He hated guns and this was his last defence.

A tingle of excitement began to creep over me with this last find. With each new discovery the true merit of my father unravelled. I wanted to go there and see for myself what a real rainforest was like. The Eden Project was a wonder of modern initiative and science. To me it was a day job to close the door on every night and forget at weekends. This was different. The more I read my father's notes and matched up the photographs, the stronger became the urge to visit the site of those images he had captured with a click of his Leica; he could have ridiculed me, I was a part timer. I put all the photographs and notes back in the briefcase. They would all go with me, especially the Swiss knife.

I suddenly felt small in my own eyes. He had been fifty or so when I was a lad at school and to me an old man. He never played games with me and was more like other boys' grandads. We were never close: he never put his arm around me when he came down to see me. He shook my hand when he left, not even a peck on the cheek. He was a boring, old businessman whom I lived with till he sent me to prep school. His adventurous side had never emerged. I would have been so proud of him. The only question in my mind was why? Why did he never let his adventures be known? He was never reticent about his courtroom victories. Perhaps I'll never know unless the answer was in the Brazilian rainforest. I had to go there.

I was so intrigued I went through the contents again trying to match each picture with one of his notes till I felt I was there. But it was only a theoretical solution in my head; I was baffled with scenes I had never imagined from geography lessons, or in my present job. Before that day was out I had already made up my mind. The money I had inherited could make it all a reality; I had no excuses to chicken out. When I drove to Cornwall two days later, I was already figuring out the how and when. I vowed to follow in his footsteps and journey to Manaus. This was the one name that was repeated several times and was obviously the real starting point for his journey.

Before I finally left the house and its secrets, some solved, but even more unanswered, I drove to the cemetery and stood once more before the black marble headstone. My emotions were completely different from two days earlier and my throat tightened to prevent tears. I tried to convey my new feelings through the cold soil covered by grey gravel. As a non-Christian I couldn't even pretend that he would hear me. I would have to be my own salvation. Peace of mind would only come when I stood before those natives as he had. It was a challenge from the grave.

Chapter 4

It's six months since I drove away from the old house in Ripon with mixed emotions. The satisfaction of my inheritance and my future finances taken care of still gives me a great feeling. It was three months before all the loose ends of the will had been finalised and a settlement figure was reached. Joseph Wilmott had detailed all this and my bank account grew accordingly. I had no regular girlfriend but was dating one of the girls from Eden. Her name was Elly Mortimer. We didn't always work together; more often than not she preferred the outside gardens. She shared a flat in St Austell with a girl called Madge, whom she'd met at college. Madge worked in St Austell and had a boyfriend. Their flat was only a five-minute drive from mine so I offered to drive her home each night. A staff minibus picked her up in the morning and she insisted on still using that. I was glad about that, I didn't fancy waiting around in the traffic of St Austell in the holiday season with all the double yellow lines. She appreciated the lift home and we struck up a friendship. I'm sure it could have been more. She was attractive and conversation came easy to us. We mostly talked shop, as we were both interested in what went on at Eden.

I thought it best not to get involved with Elly before my intended journey to South America. Any other time, I would have dated her but because we worked together, I had reservations. If for some reason it didn't work out it could have been awkward.

The girls had no commitments to each other and no parents to keep an eye on them, but I didn't want complications at this stage.

Sharing the flat with a friend was a financial plus for both girls; rents were pretty steep in St Austell, as I'd found out. The girls were independent and it also halved the chores. To have a friend at work suited me fine. I knew no one else there.

I didn't tell her about my inheritance. We were just good friends. Nevertheless, when the probate was finalised I asked her out a few times. By then I had the feeling she expected it. When I could see she liked good food and was knowledgeable about wines, I started splashing out on meals in good restaurants, and there are plenty of those in St Austell. Our evenings out became more frequent and when I paid the bill with hardly a glance at the bottom line, it was not surprising Ella gave me an *old-fashioned look*. I think she suspected a hidden agenda behind my largesse.

She knew my salary at the Eden Project didn't cover such extravagance. My free-spending attitude surprised her somewhat, but she didn't object. I hadn't tried anything on and I knew from our general conversation that I would get short thrift. I thought it necessary to ease her mind after we enjoyed a particularly good bottle of wine. I explained that I'd always had a good allowance from my dad. I'd told her all about him and his generosity. I didn't mention my inheritance. *The larger the amount, the more handsome becomes the heir. It was either W. C. Fields or Oscar Wilde who said that, from memory. In any case it's pretty obvious.*

'Now I also have my salary,' I said. 'I think I inherited his taste for the best,' I went on. 'There's nothing wrong with my libido, but I'm not trying to seduce you. You're too smart for that, Elly. You're my only friend here and I like taking you out. Things are OK between us and let's keep it that way. It could get better or it could get worse. That's in the future; let's enjoy it now. I think you already know my beliefs. I believe in Fate not the Almighty.' She smiled to say she understood. As I dropped her off later, she kissed me on the cheek.

'Thank you, Martin, for a lovely night out.'

One Saturday we went to Plymouth for the day and eventually I drove the two of us as far as Torquay. Again it was a Saturday and the sun shone throughout. We had lunch at a table outside a café with a couple of glasses of cold lager each. Then in the afternoon we went shopping. Elly bought some perfume for herself and another for her flatmate; it was Madge's birthday the following week. The men's section was next to it and she picked up an aftershave tester. She sprayed the back of her hand with it and stroked my chin with it.

'Do you like that?' She said in a matter-of fact way.

I rubbed my chin and smelled the result and said,

'Yes, it's quite good.'

She bought it before I could stop her.

'That's for a lovely day, Martin. And for all those other lovely days we've had recently.'

We stayed on the beach much longer than we intended and it seemed most of the other visitors did too. The restaurants were pretty full and when we finally had our meal it was quite late. We drank a bottle of Merlot between us, and what with the hot sun and those two beers I felt a little flushed. She noticed it too and looked a little worried about me driving back to St Austell. I suggested we find a hotel for the night.

'I'll get twin beds if you want, Elly,' I said, 'but I think it would be better than risking driving back tonight.'

So far I'd gotten no further than a bit of groping when we were a bit tipsy. It had never come to anything because of that. She was different from some of the girls at Oxford and more mature of course. I didn't want to spoil that friendship. I'd never tried getting her drunk or pestering her about it. It wouldn't have worked anyway. Always at the back of my mind was my eventual departure to South America and I didn't want to get involved.

She agreed with that old-fashioned look and smiled at the corner of her mouth as if to say, 'Who are you trying to fool, Martin?'

We found a hotel a hundred yards off the sea front near the Torquay Bowling Club. A twin was available and I registered as Mr and Mrs Lockwood. The manager was on duty and he gave me a strange look, as if doubting my masculinity: two young people asking for twin beds? It was no skin off his nose so he handed me the key. It had been a wonderful day and we had both thoroughly enjoyed it.

By the time we went up to the room I had sobered up enough to fancy at least trying get Elly to put the two beds together. In spite of sharing the bottle of wine, Ella wasn't seduced by my overtures. I was glad when I returned her to St Austell on Sunday night unsullied. I liked her as a friend and I could tell she wanted to know me as one too. If she fancied me, it wouldn't be in a hotel on a dirty weekend.

Nevertheless, I was still troubled by the occasional twinges of conscience, mostly for not telling Elly about my intended future trip to Brazil. I would eventually, of course, but at that moment I didn't feel obligated to her. At least I had a clear conscience after Torquay.

My life up to that point had been so easy and now I was getting pangs of conscience about other people – first my father and now Elly. Where will it end? Would I begin to get a furrowed brow?

Guilt had never been on my CV. Selfishness had come naturally to me and I'd always taken advantage of the circumstances. This honest assessment disturbed me for the first time in my life. Luckily Fate and a wink from the devil that is in all of us, took a hand.

Elly's friend, Madge, and her boyfriend went on holiday to Spain; I volunteered to drive them to Exeter airport and pick them up on their return. It wasn't a selfless offer, my libido needed satisfying and at last it saw a yawning opportunity with the absence of Madge for a week.

We'd been out as a foursome a couple of times and it was nothing out of my way. It would be a bit of a squash in my small car with the luggage so Ella stayed back at the flat. When I returned she had lunch ready for me as a thank you for taking them to the airport. She was always grateful for my chauffeuring her home from work each night and this generous offer towards her flatmate seemed to soften her feelings towards me. In her eyes I always seem to be doing good deeds.

Remembering my propriety in Torquay, Elly said it would be easier for me if I stayed over each night. I could use Madge's room and there was a small plot at the back of the flat where I could park my car. It would save the trouble of having to drive back to my digs, she said. And of course we could go to work together in the morning each day.

We therefore had the flat to ourselves for that week and became closer and even domestic. We spent a few of the evenings in and around St Austell eating in restaurants, and the other evenings Elly would cook dinner and I would pop and fetch a bottle of wine to go with it.

After the first of these nights – Saturday in fact – I anticipated I would be occupying Madge's bed and was surprised when Elly said we could share hers. I thought this was to avoid leaving traces that I'd stopped there and I expected the same sort of heavy petting that had occurred in Torquay. We'd been out, had a good meal and a decent bottle of red, nothing unusual in that. But I noticed a subtle difference in her attitude on our return to the flat. She was laughing more than usual and kissing and touching my face. She remarked on my aftershave, the one she'd bought me in Torquay. Moreover, she was making all the moves first. I was not a naïve student anymore; I could read the signs. It was very nice and I felt lucky.

We had a coffee and after that it was Elly who suggested it was time for bed. She touched my hand when she said it and looked into my eyes. My pulse raced a little. Had I detected the signals properly? Indeed I had.

'You go first, Martin, I think I'll have a shower before I join you.' If I needed conformation, this was it. With that in mind, I too spent some time on my ablutions. I opened the door of the lounge and told her I'd finished in the bathroom. My boxers were already slightly distorted with the possible thought of what I'd prepared it for. I think Elly noticed it. She smiled towards it and said, 'I won't be long, Martin.'

I went to the bedroom and switched the bedside lamp on. It focussed on the familiar square of a condom. I didn't need it in writing. There was a slight throbbing in my temple area. *Say no more.*

The sex was pleasurable and, virgin or not, she was never awkward. The rest of the week was idyllic and I hoped Madge and Tony got as much pleasure from their Spanish holiday.

Of course, by the end of the week our friendship had disappeared to be replaced by a closer feeling, as if we were joined at the hip. The following Monday as we drove to work, she touched my thigh and her comments were mostly bedroom. Her female hormones were kicking in and a slight cold feeling was creeping into my stomach. She was already thinking bridesmaids, honeymoon and children. I was thinking Whoa. The inevitable finally hit me as I worked in the humid atmosphere of the South American simulation at Eden. This is what it was all about for me at the moment. It was time to put my cards on the table before the banns were read. I answered visitor's questions in a daze that morning. I tended the plants with less tender care.

We met up for lunch and I could see immediately that Elly had only one thing on her mind: marriage. She was walking on air and she kissed me lovingly in the middle of the cafeteria.

I nipped it in the bud before I started eating. I told her about my proposed time off to search the Amazon rainforests and retrace my father's journey. I said it coldly as if I hadn't noticed her changed attitude. Her expression changed and froze as if I'd pressed the pause button. I went into my excuses before she had time to recover.

'I'm sorry, Elly, but I should have explained all this to you before.' I went into more detail about my father passing away and my trip up to the family home. Her expression didn't change and I knew I would have to go into overdrive.

'It was a sad occasion and I didn't tell you because we were having such a good time and you looked so happy. I didn't want to spoil it.' I told her about the camera and the photographs. I said I had been tormented about not being closer to him and wanting to find out where he'd been. I had to elaborate.

'Going there had been a daydream, Elly, a fancy. It was only recently that I decided to go there and see for myself.' I pointed to the dome through the window of the cafeteria, theatrically, I suppose, for effect.

'Can you imagine seeing what's in there for as far as the eye can see in every direction? You are the first to know about what I've decided and I'm sorry if you think I don't care about you, I do, Elly. However long it takes me I want to come back here. I want to see you again. I've never felt this way about a girl before. I know we both had a wonderful time last week and you looked so happy. I don't want to spoil that now. I hope you understand and have no regrets, Elly. Please tell me that?'

Before she had time to reply, I gave her an emotional version of my trip to the cemetery and what it would mean to me if I could follow in my father's footsteps. I mentioned I had inherited a few thousand and that's why it was possible to go on this personal journey. 'I couldn't do it otherwise. It's why we've had those lovely times together. You enjoyed them too, didn't you?'

Her silence and almost hostile look when I began was gradually replaced by a more sympathetic attitude when she spoke. She seemed slightly impressed by my resolve towards the end, and nodded. I pressed on with my enthusiasm.

'Don't you see, Elly? It's like the Eden Project without the domes. I have to go there and see it for myself. I have enough money to finance the trip; otherwise I would have had to stay here frustrated all my life.'

I continued in the same vein and before lunch was over, I could see I had won her round to my logic. I put my hand on hers across the table and kissed her affectionately. 'I do love you, Elly, you know that.' She softened and kissed me back.

'I do understand, Martin; it's just that I thought we are so good together. I had such plans for the future. I suppose I was too hasty. Do you think you'll ever come back to Cornwall, Martin?'

'Of course, Elly.' I kissed her on the lips once more, not ardently but not brotherly. 'I love Cornwall and hope they'll have me back at Eden. You will be the first person I will look up when I return. If you are married I will understand. If not I shall date you and hope we can continue where we left off. You are certainly not the reason for my leaving. All my plans were on hand before our week together. I hadn't crossed the T's or dotted the I's but I never thought I'd fall in love in such a short time, if that's what it is; but it must be. I've never felt like this before with anyone.' When I said this she looked as happy as I remember when I woke up beside her in her flat.

Our normal friendship resumed for the rest of the lunch hour and she asked me more about my plans. I told her everything I'd planned up to that point and even asked her advice. I was pleased with the way things went and she wasn't bitter towards me. At least I had been honest about my feelings for her and I had no regrets regarding that. It's just that marriage had never come into the equation. It was unfortunate that I hadn't confided in Elly about my plans before. It was selfish I know, but that's what I'd always been. What Martin wants, Martin should have.

Without telling Elly, my boss or anyone at work, I had researched all I could about northern Brazil, the Amazon and all its environs until I was satisfied I could travel to Manaus with at least a rough idea of what I was letting myself in for. Manaus would be my first target from which I intended to retrace the journey my father had made. I knew I had to see, feel and smell the atmosphere that was missing from those black and white stills. I wanted to know what he had experienced and understand what he had been through. Unfortunately, I'd just played my cards close to my chest.

During the afternoon I knocked on the door of Mr Shapiro's office. He was the head of my department and the next hurdle to climb over. I thought it best to tell him before word got to him. I asked him to accept a month's notice. He was rather surprised as he thought I had settled in nicely and enjoyed working there. I explained my reason just as I had done to Elly. He seemed to understand and I was glad that he, too, was as sympathetic to my personal ambitions. I was certainly beginning to appreciate people more. I took them both into my confidence fully the next day.

I showed Mr Shapiro and Elly the photographs and notes and my enthusiasm was obvious. My boss was quite impressed. At least he was quite impressed with what my dad had achieved. I think my determination showed through.

'I think working here has played a large part in wanting to see the real thing. I don't expect my job to be available when I return,' I said, 'but I hope when I've experienced what my father went through all those years ago it would help me get things in perspective. I really like working here, Mr Shapiro, and will apply for a position again when and if I return.' He wished me luck and hoped to see me again.

'Perhaps you'll be able to give us one or two tips when you return,' he said, probably tongue in cheek. Nevertheless I felt we'd parted on friendly terms.

For the four weeks I remained at the Eden Project I continued to take Ella home from work. We dated as we did in the days before that that idyllic week when I stayed there. It was purely platonic and I understood why. Despite winning her over, she knew that while I had been thrusting I had had my sights on South America. But we were still friends; she didn't hold a grudge. Perhaps it was because I still took her home every night till I left. Then maybe I'm still cynical.

I went to my doctor for a check-up just to make sure I was fit enough to stand the rigours of what lay ahead. I told him where I was going and the number of injections he prescribed left me in no doubt as to what sort of diseases lay in wait. This would be no holiday in Spain. I spent considerable time and money on my outfit. A pith helmet and shorts were out, I decided. My father certainly looked the intrepid explorer but his appearance was not for me. Light denim trousers and jacket seemed in order. It's what the modern TV explorer appeared to favour. Waterproofs that guaranteed to breathe a little and a khaki baseball cap completed my purchases in that department. I took further advice from my doctor regarding a small supply of tropical medications and added these from the pharmacist. I hoped to get further advice if I engaged the services of a local guide, and I certainly intended doing that. I saw no such guide in the old photos, but I thought one would be essential. I'd keep my options open of course, but local knowledge would lessen my apprehension. In the diaries my father had mentioned several episodes of fevers, stomach upsets and bites from various insects that hovered, waiting to pounce on non-native victims. These notes were written almost tongue-in-cheek in a stiff upper lip manner. I'm sure the conditions would be harsher than he made out. The notes were short and to the point, with no elaboration. He described the heat and humidity in clinical terms with temperatures, and an assessment of the humidity. It was all written as if preparing a brief; as if he was practicing his future skills and didn't want to bore the jury or his Lordship. As I read it, his voice superimposed my thoughts. In other words, he hadn't gilded the lily. He probably underplayed the severity of it all.

Every morning waking up prior to leaving I would experience doubts about my sanity. Even as I slept I thought of something I might need. It was worse than waiting to go on any holiday I'd ever been on. On the Costas I could at least pop into a shop for forgotten items.

As the last of my connecting planes touched down at Belém airport I already had misgivings. It had been a long and tiring journey with numerous hiccups for all sorts of reasons. And this, I supposed, was the easy part, in the comfort of an air-conditioned aircraft. I made enquiries at the desk regarding the next part of my journey. There were two flights a day to Manaus, I was informed, and of course I had missed the second one. I couldn't buy a ticket for it at the airport anyway, so I made my way to the exit.

There were a few taxis lined up outside the airport and I finally found one where the driver spoke a little English. This would be another drawback. I should have learned a little more Portuguese than the few banal words I had rehearsed so diligently. They may be OK for the staff of hotels and restaurants but would be of little use where I would end up.

Although suitably dressed, even the taxi driver was perspiring. The humidity was more than I was used to even when on holiday abroad. I said I wanted a reasonably good hotel in the centre of town. I think he got the drift and fifteen minutes later we entered the Avenida Presidente Vargas. He stopped outside the Itaoca and gave me an enquiring shrug of the shoulders and I got out. I paid him. That had been reasonably civilised, despite my wariness of taxi drivers in general.

I walked up the wide steps to the reception. It looked fairly modern, central and quite near the docks, I observed. Whether it was in town I had no idea. I registered and paid with cash; cards were not acceptable, I was informed with a simple shake of the head. The girl behind the desk was quite smart but not conversational in any language. I was not in the mood to pursue any further enquiries and tired after the flight. I'd eaten on the plane and didn't feel the need anyway to risk food in a strange hotel on my first night.

I went to my room and dumped my luggage at the side of the bed. It looked clean and comfortable and, after a few minutes fiddling, the overhead fan whirred into motion. It was noisy but I reasoned that would prevent me hearing mosquitoes as they honed in on me and may send me to sleep. The towels were clean and I freshened up a little. I went back to the reception and the girl pointed me in the direction of the bar when I made a drinking motion. With my luck today, I was surprised it was open. There were only two other occupants and apart from speaking Portuguese they could have been two similar businessmen in a British hotel, talking shop. I had a couple of drinks at the bar and went to bed. The room was quite comfortable and the hotel itself modern. The overhead fan was still working and seemed noisier. I didn't turn it off. It drowned out the traffic noise and in the end lulled me to sleep. It was a fitful sleep and I woke several times. I itched in several places and hoped it was from bed bugs and not various insects that I would eventually come to fear and respect. The toilet had more than its fair share of the winged creatures when I used it. Their next port of call would be the kitchen. I tried not to think about such things, and in the course of the next few weeks would learn to accept the consequences.

It was a continental breakfast and quite appetising. The hotel manager was on duty when I left and he gave me a street map of Belém. I set off to walk into the centre of the city. The heat was intense already. I strolled gently, keeping to the shadow of buildings. It took me half an hour to reach the business area and I vowed to return by taxi, there would be plenty here. I had made arrangements at my bank before leaving so I could have access to money on my travels. I had deposited ten thousand pounds in a debit account. I hoped that between that and my credit card I would be without any financial problems. My father would have been without such luxuries. I gave my debit card a try out the next morning at the first Banco do Brasil I came across, obtaining two thousand pounds worth of Real. I would keep five hundred in my wallet and distribute the rest about my person and equipment so as to not have all my eggs in one basket. I didn't want to expose large sums at a time when I needed it. Where I was going, even small amounts were more than most of the people I'd come in contact with would see in a lifetime. I had no intention of putting ideas in their heads.

There were several travel agents and I had no idea of their individual reputations so I negotiated an airline ticket with the one who had the best English-speaking assistant. I got one-way of course; I didn't want to be too over-confident in case Fate was listening. The flight wasn't till tomorrow morning. He neatly put the tickets in an envelope and wrote down all the necessary details for my benefit for when I reached the airport on the outside. He certainly put me at my ease.

Although I had read as much as I could before I came about the places I would be visiting, I couldn't believe the quality of the architecture here. Most of the Victorian and Georgian housing had survived the steamy summers and torrential rains. History had not been one of my best subjects and I'd always imagined South American countries as backward with very little culture. How wrong I'd been. No expense had been spared when the city was at its richest, during the rubber boom in the late nineteenth and early twentieth century. With cheap labour, entrepreneurial Europeans had money to spare on a lavish lifestyle. A lot of the old Georgian colonial buildings remained much in evidence and the best materials had been imported from Europe. Now of course there were a spate of modern glass and concrete blocks alongside.

Because of the size of Brazil there are great fluctuations in the weather. I had opted for September, as it's the driest time of the year in Amazonas, in theory that is. Even so, I knew general forecasts couldn't be trusted. This much I'd learned from my father's notes. Forewarned is forearmed so I expected more than a British April shower. It will still be hot and humid and very wet, I've no doubt.

Belém was hot, but as it's on the Atlantic coast, a cool breeze took away some of the humidity, except in the centre of the city. I expected Manaus to be more tropical. Brazil is huge in anyone's imagination and its statistics are mind-blowing. At Oxford I'd taken little notice of subjects that weren't necessary for my academic advancement. Geography was one of them and so I brushed up on the statistics of Brazil before setting off on my expedition. It occupies half the landmass of South America and is the fifth largest country in the world. It has over four thousand miles of coast on the Atlantic side and its inland borders join all the other South American countries except Chile and Ecuador. It has every sort of terrain except desert and high mountains and has the largest river system in the world. It also has the largest rainforest. The gloomy ecologists said this wouldn't last as it was being exploited. I'm of the opinion that the earth looks after itself. It managed to survive every sort of weather condition for millions of years and, despite an ever-changing population of flora, fauna and creatures of every description, it's still here. But maybe I'm wrong and man and his selfish greed is its final nemesis.

Situated below the Amazon estuary, Belém is where the Rio Tocantins enters the Atlantic. The hotel manager who gave me the street map was more forthcoming than the receptionist. He politely asked the reason for my visit and seemed genuinely interested. When I explained, he knew I wasn't just another tourist passing through and would welcome any information that wasn't in the guidebooks. He gave me a brief history of Belém. In fairly good English he explained that imports from all over the world arrived there and it was from where exports from northern Brazil were sent. Ocean-going vessels could reach as far as Manaus and beyond, which is another thousand miles along the Amazon westwards. I stopped him as he said this. I explained that this was as if a ship entered the Thames in London and sailed through to Scotland and beyond. The more I learnt about Brazil the more I realised how small Britain is.

He pointed out places of interest on the map and circled them. He had suggested a visit to the Museum Emilio Goeldi if I had time. Satisfied that my financial arrangements were in order and the flight tickets secured, I decided I had time to see as much of the city as I could.

I joined a few tourists from various parts of the world, Americans and Japanese amongst them, of course. The information desk coped with all my questions. I learned that Belém had the largest cathedral in northern Brazil. It had a

University, a teacher training school, a classical theatre and even an institute for the research of tropical diseases. So here I was, in a city I had never heard of in all of my academic life. It had buildings as beautiful as in Bath or Edinburgh say, with a high cultural background and much going for it. It was not the backwater place I had expected. And I would be further surprised later.

I spent the morning tracking down some the main places of interest that I'd been made aware of at the information desk. My digital camera clicked madly. I would have the chance to edit them tonight in the hotel. At least I would be sure of some good photographs when I returned home. I made notes at the same time to correspond accordingly. This was the beginning of my journal, although I didn't expect it to be this easy in the future. Still, if I could return to Cornwall with some sort of a record of these and subsequent places and events I'd be satisfied.

As my flight wasn't till tomorrow, I intended seeing as much of the city as I could today. I didn't know if I would return this way even if I survived! I am a confirmed optimist but I didn't want to tempt fate by assuming too much. I may be an atheist but the Devil in the form of ill luck is realistic, and it's always trying to catch the unwary out.

Again, I was surprised how modern Belém looked yet still retaining these old buildings. There were similarities between it and cities in Spain and Portugal, with plazas and public gardens. Here, the squares were Praças and the largest was the Praça da República, naturally. It's not just a square, it has a tree-lined park and that's where I headed. In the centre is the impressive Teatro da Paz – the Theatre of Peace, I guessed.

I carried the small, waterproof satchel containing my father's records with me all the time and never let it out of my sight. It was a reminder of his achievements. I intended to refer to it during my own journey and I hoped it would be a spur if I ever got despondent or felt like giving up. It was a comfort blanket. It also held my own digital camera and a supply of SD cards. I added the grand opera house, with its nineteenth century splendour and Rococo architecture. Although there were no pictures taken by him of Belém, I imagined him standing here all those years ago. Of course, the burger bars and other twentieth century shops surrounding me were a bit of a let-down so I contrived to keep them out of shot as much as possible. I was enjoying my day of sightseeing but didn't kid myself. This was the icing of a cake with unknown ingredients below the surface. I must make the most of it. It may be one of the few pleasant memories of my trip; I was determined to savour what was on offer.

Though it was quite hot, the occasional breeze from the Atlantic made it pleasant and the shade from the trees helped. I had a snack in one of the many cafés in the square and, even though I knew the coming weeks would probably be unpleasant in comparison, I enjoyed that first taste of Brazil. Culturally it seemed to have a great colonial past, and it was a day to remember. Whatever else happened, this was worth remembering.

The flight to Manaus was less than four hours and I was in for more surprises when I arrived there. The city is the capital of the state of Amazonas and is on the north side of the Rio Negro, just above the confluence of where the Rio Negro and the Rio Solimões meet to form the Amazon River. The Negro is black and the Solimões is brown and such is the force and magnitude of the waters, they run side by side without mixing for six kilometres. I found out this and much more later. The city is in the middle of the rainforest and ideally located for where I intended to set off, that much I did know. This is where my father's journey really began, and all the contents of his battered briefcase start here.

Manaus is on a plateau overlooking the river and is dissected by several *canoe* channels dividing it up into departments. *Canoe* is a misnomer as some of these waterways are as big as rivers in Britain. The city looked even bigger than Belém from the air, probably because it has spread out with the recent industrial developments. I learned from the hotel manager in Belém that there had always been a rivalry between the two cities over the centuries. This increased after 1900 when rubber became an important commodity worldwide due to the industrial revolution, especially the car industry, of course. The main source of rubber up to that time was the Brazilian rainforests. Countries in the Far East saw the opportunity. I read that it was an Englishman who took the first seeds of the rubber trees from here and they ended up in the Far East, Malaya and Burma etc, where the climate was suitable. In a few years, most of the rubber came from there. It was easier to transport it from those places than the likes of Manaus and Belém. They quickly lost out and their main source of income declined.

Now of course, both of the cities are flourishing, thanks to foreign investments in diverse industries. One of the largest exports is timber, unfortunately this is having a disastrous effect on the rainforests. Manaus is much more commercial than Belém. It refines the oil brought down from Peru by barge and manufactures a wide range of products. I learned they have a Tax Free Zone and that most of the electronics are made here for Brazil. Merchant ships take these across the world. These facts were going round in my mind before we had landed.

I immediately noticed the increase in humidity as I walked down the steps from the plane. I was surprised to learn later that there is a natural jungle park on the outskirts. There are also botanical and zoological gardens. It must be like the tropical sections of the Eden Project, without the domes. There's a certain irony there. Perhaps I should avoid visiting it. It may give me a false impression of what to expect. It may also deter me from continuing my journey.

Before arriving, Manaus was mostly a mystery to me, despite my enquiries. I knew it was the capital of Amazonas, which is the largest state in Brazil and covers 605,000 square miles. That's more than six times the size of the UK. There are only two million people in the state and *half of those live in Manaus*. To put this in perspective, there are almost four times more people in London than in the whole of the state. It also means there's a lot of uninhabited rainforest to get lost in.

The tourist office at Belém had given me a list of hotels for Manaus and a Brazilian businessman from Rio de Janeiro overheard my enquiries and suggested one he'd stayed at regularly. I won't name it because of later events. So far, strangers I'd met had been very helpful and had smoothed out my progress. I hoped my luck would continue. A taxi took me to this hotel and I gave him the required Reals, which was no more than five pounds even with a tip. I began to think taxi drivers are much maligned. My inherent distrust of foreigners in general began to melt.

I went through the usual formalities of registering without any problems and proceeded up to my room in the lift. The hotel was not far from the port. This was added information from the man who had recommended it. It was only a short distance from the docks where small riverboats collect for the use of adventurous tourists. This would be my goal and where I intended to start my journey proper.

My room was on the third floor and overlooked the Praça dos Remedos. As I exited the lift I caught my first glimpse of the Rio Negro from a large glass window. I intended taking full advantage of the hotel's comforts as I made final preparations for my forthcoming expedition. Again, there were no complaints after I settled into the room. I saw little point in changing shirts every time I changed hotels. The freshness didn't last long anyway. I had a shower and applied plenty of deodorant and aftershave. The restaurant was air-conditioned and I could have been on the Algarve in Portugal as I listened to the other diners. I ate a delightful meal with a couple of glasses of wine. During the evening Lady Luck smiled on me once more as I enjoyed an excellent meal of fish; I didn't enquire about its origin. In the rivers, there are some 1,500 identified species of fish, including many types of piranha, electric eels, and over four hundred species of catfish. I could be eating any of them. It tasted delicious.

During the meal I became aware of the couple at a nearby table. Unlike the majority of diners this was a business dinner; that much I could tell by certain words. One of them was an American and, it transpired, represented a Pittsburgh engineering company. The other owned a factory in Manaus and was Portuguese. They were discussing construction work the latter needed. Most of it went over my head, but the conversation was mostly in English. I didn't want to interrupt their business deal so I bided my time. When I considered they'd concluded the job in hand and were chatting about the usual family affairs, I seized my opportunity.

'I hope you don't mind if I break into your conversation,' I began, 'but perhaps one of you gentlemen may be able to help me.' The Brazilian raised his eyebrows and cautiously remained silent. The American, of course, was glad to hear someone speaking English and broke into a smile.

'Cain't promise, fella, but let's have it.'

I told them my name, said where I was from and gave a brief outline of what I had in mind, even showing them a photograph or two from my dad's collection. It was the American who spoke again, as I expected. As a salesman he was used to talking to strangers and pointed to a vacant chair at their table. His companion's face softened a little and nodded in agreement.

'Sit yourself down, Martin,' he said affably, 'but I think Philippe here is more likely to be the guy you're looking for.' He looked expectantly towards the other man at the table hopefully. The Brazilian eyed me up and down a little sceptically. *What I had in mind seemed a little ambitious for a young, pale-skinned Briton.* He'd listened with a slightly bemused expression as I spoke, but I could see the photos had intrigued him. His dark eyes surveyed me, and my newly acquired clothes. I could see he already doubted my sanity. With his long, wavy hair and black goatee beard he was every inch a descendent of some Portuguese pirate-ship captain. At least my imagination said so. A smile appeared at the corner of his mouth and his eyes glinted in amusement.

'I hope you have come well-prepared, Martin.' He rolled the R in my name and pronounced it Martine. His English, or I should say American, was excellent; no doubt he had been educated at an American university.

'You say you are in need of a guide and possibly two porters for your proposed trip. It is possible; I know someone for the first and he will no doubt be able to supply you with the second if they are necessary. And any other needs for such a journey. There are plenty of young men in Manaus who will jump at the chance to carry your supplies; this man I can assure you will see you are dealt with honestly.'

He took out a business card with his company's logo and his own name on the bottom. He scribbled something on the back in Portuguese with a flourish and handed it to me.

'Maybe you take a taxi from the hotel tomorrow afternoon to this address. Arrive at three o'clock. Show the back of the card to the receptionist and she will contact me in my office.' I was taken aback by his generous response. He was obviously a successful businessman and used to making quick decisions. He went on.

'One of my employees has a nephew who is called José. He has a thirty-foot canoe and takes small groups on expeditions northwards up the Rio Negro. He probably knows more about that part of the river than anyone and I think that is where these photographs were taken. He's been exploring the river all his life. He started as a lad working on one of the many supply boats that deliver to the villages. His uncle says he became bored with the daily routine. Now he has his own boat and enjoys showing tourists out-of-the-way places – and there are many where you will be going. You will also see many more species of the rainforest than the normal tourist if I am not mistaken. I will see to it that his uncle contacts him and asks if he would be available for such a venture. By three o'clock I should know.'

Once more I couldn't believe my luck. I only hoped it wouldn't be dashed down just around the corner. I thanked Philippe and his American companion for their help. The Portuguese businessman brushed aside my enthusiasm.

'I hope you are aware of what you may be letting yourself in for, Martin. But I suppose if you have travelled all this way it is more than a whim. If it's true your father completed a similar journey, then perhaps you have his resolution, good luck to you. If after talking to José you have second thoughts, you could take the tour of the jungle park on the outskirts of the city. You could take many photographs in there and they would look pretty authentic to your friends when you return home.' He went into detail of what was on offer there. He told me the full name of the research institute, but it was too much for me to remember. Its initials were INPA. He grinned and his dark eyes glinted mischievously. 'It will certainly be cheaper too.'

He still seemed to have his doubts about my determination. At the end of our chat, I think Arnie the American was a little envious of *this mad Limey*, as he remarked to his friend. The waiter came over to see if drinks were needed.

Philippe excused himself. He and Arnie had concluded their business deal and he was expected home for dinner with his family. He hoped to see me tomorrow, he said before he left.

I ordered two drinks for Arnie and myself and we talked about our families and respective home lives. He also confirmed that Philippe was a straight dealer and that I could trust him.

'There are no contracts,' he said. 'I'll fly back tomorrow and all the paperwork will be as we agreed. Never had a problem yet with him.' He rose from his chair.

'I should be hitting the hay, Martin. I have an early flight tomorrow.' He shook my hand in a tight grip. 'Best of luck.' And he was off.

I was quite pleased with my progress in what little time I'd been here. The discomforts of the past twenty-four hours faded at least for the present. The night was still young and the restaurant was deserted. I went into the bar. It had comfortable leather chairs and was easier on the eye than my room. Two large fans in the ceiling kept the room at a comfortable ambience. The television was showing the inevitable football match. I decided to pass the time away watching it and having just a couple more drinks before bedtime. There was no sound on the TV and speakers around the room issued recordings of gentle Brazilian music. I'd make the most of these comforts; I could be a long time without them. The only other occupants were a family of four locals. They appeared to consist of a young married couple and the parents of one of them celebrating a special night out, maybe a birthday or an anniversary. They regularly took pictures to mark the occasion. I watched them closely, not understanding what they were saying but somehow guessing that they were a happy family; something I'd never experienced. I felt envious of them and a little homesick paradoxically, as I'd no family to go home to. Here was I surrounded by foreigners, yet with my insular attitude there was no one I longed to return to. I felt lonely. The glass of local beer did little to put me out of this mood so I asked for a *Cuba livre,* hoping the white rum would help. I think it was nearly a hundred percent proof, for it did its job. I mellowed very quickly. A couple of Brazilian girls came in and I was surprised that they were unaccompanied. They weren't young; about thirty I guessed, but with good figures and well dressed. They smiled in my direction when they came in, their teeth showing white against their dark skins. It was some time since my last sexual experience on holiday and since then I had been too busy, absorbed in preparing for my forthcoming expedition. Now the strong spirit reminded me of my celibacy and as I continued to admire these two lovelies I became slightly aroused. I had experienced something similar in England when drinking rum. It always tends to relax my morals, or indeed pervert them. I went to the bar for a refill with one thing on my mind. As I passed their table the spirit spoke for me.

'*Nao Homem?*' it said before I had time to bite my tongue. One of the girls answered in excellent English. She smiled and there was no sign I had caused any offence. I was relaxed enough to dispense with the Dutch courage of the rum.

'We are both divorced,' she said, which not only answered the question but explained the reason they were unaccompanied, and their maturity. Speaking my language was an unexpected bonus. My spirit-fuelled brain raced into top gear.

'Could I buy you both a drink? I'm a lonely Englishman and this is my last night before heading for the rain forests and the comforts of civilisation.' I said it as if I had been condemned to Devil's Island penal colony for a life sentence. My furrowed brow encouraged sympathy. It was the same girl who answered. It was she who had a superb mastery of the English language.

'Of course,' she said, 'perhaps you could bring your chair over to our table. I am sure we would both be interested to hear your reasons for going on such an arduous journey. It would certainly be more interesting than the football match.'

I didn't hesitate and did as I was told. Two glasses of wine were in order, she said, and I fetched them from the bar, together with another white rum for myself. The barman smiled as he placed the drinks in front of me and gave an almost imperceptible wink. With his experience, he could read my inner thoughts. I feigned innocence as if nothing was further from my mind.

The girls introduced themselves as Beatriz and Matilde; the former did most of the talking for the pair. Sometimes she would interpret for her friend if I talked too fast. My exuberance at being in the company of these two beautiful coffee coloured girls allowed my tongue to run away with me, the strong spirit did the rest. I embellished my story to impress them and stood to fetch more drinks for the three of us. My legs gave way slightly and I had to sit down. I felt a little woozy and apologised. I'd been drunk before and knew I'd had enough. I hoped they would excuse me, as I needed my rest for tomorrow. Beatriz said they understood, and as I staggered towards the lift, she and her friend followed me.

'We are ready for home too,' she said, 'we will help you to your room.' I thanked her for the offer, making an effort to pull myself together. I felt a little foolish and tried to shrug off the offer. The girls insisted and the perfume from their bodies was the clincher. The very nearness of them had sobered me up slightly by the time the three of us reached my room. My mind raced to think of some way of delaying their departure from my life as I opened the door; but there was no need for me to say anything. They followed me in and closed it gently.

'How would you like the pleasure of our company in your bed tonight, Martin?' It was Matilde and it was the first time she had spoken all night. My befuddled brain attempted to clear itself. These two high-class prostitutes had played me for a sucker. The hotel was their office and rich tourists were their clients. The barman was maybe in with them too on a commission. His wink should have tipped me off.

Once my ego had recovered from the duplicity I wasn't too displeased. Matilde made three mugs of coffee from the tray provided and Beatriz kept me engaged, asking about life in England. We drank the coffee and I felt a little better.

They had already assessed my potential after listening to my bravado ramblings. My tacit response to Matilde's opening question was sufficient for them to know I was agreeable for them to stay the night. Money was never mentioned; they were too well-schooled in their trade for such sordid details. Gently they went about their business. It was Beatriz who led me to the bed with her honeyed tones and where I got my first taste of females who get paid for sex. I had never needed to before. Fellow students had regaled me with their experiences and most of them agreed that it was pay up front and over very quickly. Had I been in full possession of my faculties I've no doubt it would have been the best sex I had ever enjoyed in my few short years. I'm no Casanova, so apart from the episode with Julie at her parents' house in Cornwall, my only other experiences have been after much fumbling and in unsuitable venues: a small car, wet grass etc. Elly had been different, of course.

These Brazilian beauties showed me how to make love. I do remember that and even in my state I delivered the goods. There was no embarrassment that I had felt with previous encounters with the opposite sex on these occasions.

I even remembered showering with the two girls first and they towelled me down, which was an experience in itself. I didn't even have to search awkwardly for a condom and leave the girl in limbo. All the preliminaries were taken care of. I know I finally became lost in the pleasure from the pair of them and dropped off to sleep.

Chapter 5

The bright sun's rays found a gap in the curtain and finally sought out my face. I closed the gap and dashed to the toilet. My last moments before sleep had been heaven. In those few hours after, my euphoria turned to misery. My head throbbed from the after-effects of pure white rum and last night's episode unfolded between throbs. I closed my eyes to relive it. Half a dozen conjectures hit me at the same time and my head couldn't cope. I stood under the shower and let the cold water shock my system. I stood there for an eternity wondering how stupid I'd been. Had my luck finally run out? I found a fresh towel and gave myself a good rub down trying to calm down. I decided to make a cup of coffee. I sat on the edge of the bed and imagined the worst.

My last vision of the two naked dusky maidens lingered. I could still smell their perfume from my first encounter with them in the bar downstairs. I remembered the smell of the shower gel that the three of us had shared. Towards the end of our exertions, especially mine, there had been the whiff of musk from the mingling perspirations. How much had it cost me, this experience? I tried to be philosophical about it. It was my own fault whatever the cost. I went across to my clothes that were folded neatly on a chair – certainly not my doing. I opened my wallet. At least my credit cards were still intact. I counted my money. Three hundred pounds in Real were missing, one hundred and fifty pounds each. A bargain after what I had first supposed. It could have been much worse. I could have been murdered as I slept and they could have taken everything I had, but I doubted it. You don't kill the golden goose. It would have put an end to their nice little earner. I breathed a sigh of relief. I wondered if that Rio de Janeiro businessman who recommended the hotel had made use of the services of the two girls.

I went to my suitcase and picked out fresh clothes for the day. Then I headed for the shower again. This time I let the warm water cascade all over and imagined the one last night with those two beauties. Once more I enjoyed the smell of the gel and closed my eyes. It would be a long time before I forgot Beatriz and Matilde. If I had any funds left after my travels in the jungle I could return here. *I don't think so.*

After breakfast I strolled down to the port. Once more I am amazed at what I see before me. I stand looking at a river I'd never heard of six months ago. It's almost like being on the dockside in Liverpool. The water's clear but black, giving it its name. This is due to the decomposed organic matter that seeps in from the surrounding swamps and is totally different from the Amazon that it joins in the confluence that swirls around here in Manaus. The Rio Negro originates as far away as Venezuela and Colombia and is 1400 miles long. About a third of it is navigable before it reaches the Amazon. I can see large transport vessels loading and unloading, all going to and coming from foreign ports all over the world.

Although a river port, there is so much water feeding it from its headwaters and the Amazon which it joins, that there is a rise and fall of forty feet annually, unbelievable! To cope with this there are floating wharves. It says much for the farsightedness of those early settlers from Europe that they saw the potential of the raw materials in the rainforests and took advantage of these huge rivers for transport.

I found a dockside bar. The barman had a cigar clamped between his teeth and after much discussion and sign language I sat down with the result – a baguette filled with some sort of dried ham. I had a small black coffee and a large cup half filled with hot water. I wasn't aware of any of the intimidation from the occupants that I'd read about before coming. They didn't welcome me, it was true. They drank their small black coffees and smoked their various weeds, deep in animated conversations with each other. They simply ignored me and that was OK. Perhaps it would be different at night. I didn't intend to find out. I made my way to the taxi rank.

The Barra Negro construction company is away from the city centre on a large industrial estate. This is on a raised plateau that keeps it from being flooded from the monsoonal rains. The air was humid as it had been all day. The temperature had soared into the nineties. I was wet through with sweat without any physical effort on my part. I began to imagine what it would be like when I began my journey through the rainforest. Philippe's scepticism nags away at me. To add to the discomfort, smoke and fumes from various chemical companies filled the air. I imagined workers' safety is an 'also ran' in an attempt by the bosses to compete with world competition. Money is their prime motive with little thought for workers or the environment. My taxi finally locates the Barra Negro office building and drops me there. I entered the offices and the cool air-conditioning seemed to freeze the sweat onto my back. The dark-skinned receptionist smiled as I visibly shivered. Simply by the colour of my skin and my attire she knew who I was. Philippe would have forewarned her.

She rang through to her boss even before I offered her the card. He was busy for the next ten minutes or so, she explained, and offered me a coffee. It was a small espresso accompanied by a glass of water and the strong Brazilian liquid helped ease the throbbing still pounding my head. Eventually she pointed to the lift and I finally arrived at the door of Philippe Sousa's office. He opened the door at my knock and invited me in. It could have been an office in any city in the world, with its modern furniture. He couldn't avoid noticing the damp patches on my light shirt but didn't comment. A girl came in with more coffees – after all this was Brazil. There was only one other chair in his office apart from his own. This was on the other side of his desk and he rose and offered it to me. The chair was comfortable. It would be for sales reps and the like.

I thought it prudent to ask about his business to break the ice. He seemed pleased that I seemed relaxed in his presence, despite my obvious discomfort due to the heat. He gave me a brief outline of the sort of construction work they were involved in. Most of it was for bridges that spanned the many waterways surrounding the city. Although inflation was high, Brazil was entering into a more prosperous phase in its history he said. He and his contemporaries knew it was at the expense of the ecology, but no one was willing to be the first to give it consideration. The financial rewards far outweighed the consequences for future Brazilians. It was said in a matter-of-fact way. It was an issue that was a running sore and no longer needed clarifying and he did have the excuse used by his fellow industrialists to justify their actions.

'Britain made the same sacrifices to attain its position in the great industrial revolution,' he said smiling, as if to excuse he and his fellow entrepreneurs. I had to agree with him.

He passed a sheet of paper over to me. On it was the name and address of the man he had mentioned the previous night. There was also a short CV provided by the prospective guide's uncle. It was quite reassuring and more than I could have expected, had I needed to look for one myself.

'As a stranger it would not be easy for you to find his address. To save you the trouble, I said it would be best if he called at your hotel this evening.'

I sensed that he wanted to avoid sending me into one of the run-down areas of the city, the Favelos. These were ghettoes where crime was rife, life was cheap and the police very rarely entered. It was something the new Brazil had to deal with in the near future. Strangers, especially foreigners, were easy targets. 'If not I'll pass a message on to him through his uncle for some other time that would be suitable for you.'

'No that's fine,' I said quickly. I wanted to get things moving now that I was here and couldn't see the point in hanging around.

'I can't believe my luck in meeting you, Philippe.' He seemed to have warmed to me and to be in no hurry to get rid of me. He talked more about his business. He was obviously proud of his success. He explained that it was his grandfather who had started it after working for the British at the beginning of the century. It was they who began making improvements to the port facilities and the floating docks. Before I left, he insisted on taking me on a tour of his factory. The huge workshops were making metal fabrications for bridges and the skeletons for prefabricated buildings. Conditions here were different than his office. Sweat ran down the workers bodies as they toiled, wearing very little except a safety helmet. For all his charm, Philippe had no qualms or conscience about showing me the conditions his workers endured for low wages.

He wished me luck again before I left and hoped I would call on him when I returned that way. I thanked him and asked if I could ask his receptionist to ring for a taxi to take me back. He waved his hands.

'My driver will take you back to town in my Land Rover. Perhaps when you return from your journey and have successfully reached your goal you will have coloured photographs to show me. You will be most welcome to see me without an appointment. I would like to know what it is like in the rainforest. It is somewhere I have never ventured.' He smiled when he said it. 'When my children get the urge to see what they learn about our country at school, I take them to the theme park here in the city. There are no dangers to them and we finish up at McDonalds for beef burgers afterwards.' It was said tongue-in-cheek and I laughed with him at the irony of his remarks.

Chapter 6

I must admit it was a slightly apprehensive Martin Lockwood that waited for José Barcelos to turn up. Because he was Portuguese of course, his name was pronounced almost like the English Josie and not like the Spanish Ho-say. I must remember that. The meeting had been arranged in the bar. I had dined early and already had had a couple of drinks in addition to the glass of wine with my meal. I felt I might need Dutch courage. My meeting with the Brazilian scared me. Had Philippe's offer been as friendly as it seemed? Were he and the American having a little fun at the expense of a naive Englishman? Had they saddled me with some rip-off thug who would take my money and abandon me in the middle of nowhere? All my bravado was beginning to fade as I waited.

I went through some of the things I'd researched before I came, to take my mind off the reality of the situation. Because of the sheer size of it, Brazil had drawn people from all over the world.

As in the USA and Mexico, South America had for centuries been the home for native Indians who had migrated via the Northwest Passage from Asia, when the two continents were joined. My research seemed to intimate that Portuguese Brazilians seemed to tolerate other ethnic groups, and intermarriage was more acceptable than in most other European colonies. But, as in other societies, integration has never been completely free of strife. Exploitation of the indigenous people is worldwide. Like the United States and other countries, there is a self-imposed apartheid, and some groups have chosen to remain separate from their neighbours in their social lives, mainly for their own safety when they first arrive. It had made fascinating reading and to me it seemed integration was eventually a shelter for immigrants to hide in. Unfortunately, ghettoes could become targets by larger groups when the economy is suffering. It was easy for Hitler's Nazis to target the Jews in the thirties and similar events occurred in the in the USSR. It even happens in Britain. Immigrants settle into enclaves with their own colour, race or religion. This keeps them as outsiders to the locals and creates resentment. They are also easier to spot.

In Brazil, over half the population can trace their ancestry back to Europe and, although the numbers of people of mixed ethnic origins are increasing, about two-fifths of the total are mulattoes. These are of mixed African and European ancestry. The other main group are mestiços, which are people of mixed European and Indian ancestry. Added to all this and, more recently in terms of history, immigrants have arrived from Germany, Eastern Europe and even Japan. Now it seems, the indigenous Indians who chose to remain in the hinterland are the smallest of the ethnic groups, however, as many as one-third of all Brazilians have some Indian ancestors. I had already sensed that people with lighter skin got the better jobs, and that the original native Indians came off worst. My lofty philosophical ramblings had passed the time, but were interrupted when the man I was to interview entered the lobby. There was little doubt it was he.

José Barcelos was a big man and, as he strode towards me in the hotel reception area, his mixed ancestry certainly showed through. I judged him to be in his early forties. There was something Portuguese about his facial bone structure, his nose aquiline; yet his shiny black hair, unashamedly plaited, showed Indian ancestry. Added to this and despite living in a constant thirty degrees, his skin was not as dark as I would have expected; perhaps there were genes from a German or East European antecedent. He was clean-shaven and smelled of aftershave. This would be for the interview, which meant he was a little nervous too. I was paying and he wanted the job. It made me feel more relaxed. He had a pleasant, agreeable attitude without being obsequious, tools of his trade when dealing with rich American and Japanese tourists. He would be in charge but he knew his place. I liked that.

Apart from Philippe, he was the first Brazilian I had studied up close. Philippe, of course, was mostly Portuguese; José had evolved from the various ethnic groups I'd read about. At least that was my first impression. He gave my hand a firm yet friendly shake and we sat down. Because of my slight mistrust of Philippe and the American's motive for pointing me in the direction of José, I was still wary at first. I had read enough to be warned about the places to avoid in the city; It was stressed that some of the tour operators were not to be trusted. Once in the rainforest I knew I would be at their mercy with all its dangers. My chance meeting with the

American and the Brazilian had at least saved me from having to make my own mind up from the assortment at the dockside, an unsavoury place even in daylight I was told, and to be avoided unaccompanied. Now it would be up to me to make an assessment of this prospective guide. Even so, I'd take my time before a yea or a nay and committing myself to an arduous journey with him. He sat down.

I asked him if he would like a drink and he said coffee would be fine. I signalled the waiter and ordered *dois cafés*. He took my order and disappeared. The man opposite spoke fairly good English and that seemed a bonus. I don't think my father had that luxury. Away from civilisation for any length of time it would be an advantage. He was mainly self-taught I guessed, and had cleverly learned nuances of the English language from his customers over the years. I found out later that he'd had a better education than many of his peers due to his uncle. I could tell he had gleaned as much as possible about me from his uncle via Philippe. Nevertheless as if well-rehearsed, he went into his tourist sales-pitch of what was on offer if I engaged him. The accompanying smile was part of his normal spiel. Despite this I sensed his honesty and waited till he'd finished. I smiled in a similar fashion.

'I don't know if your uncle passed on the reason for my visit here Jose?' I said and passed over the folder with all the notes and photographs from my father's effects. 'Perhaps you would look at these before we go further.'

I had decided to be quite open about what I wanted. He studied them carefully for a considerable time and the commercial smile faded. He knew about them and after scrutinising them closely, he became serious and genuinely interested in their contents. His own love of the rainforest and its inhabitants showed through as he put the last one down. His reaction was certainly not what I expected and was somewhat reassuring.

'Senhor Lockwood,' he said with genuine bewilderment, 'these photographs could have been taken last week. Although they are in black and white, I recognise where they were taken. I was born in that particular part of the forest. Little has changed since that time. Civilisation has never reached out and spoilt it. Those people are still there – I even recognise some of them. Some of the older ones have passed away of course. Some of the younger ones have left for the cities. I was one of those luckier ones.' He reminisced for a while quietly and went through the photos again comparing them to his memories and nodding at each one. He gazed into his coffee cup.

'My uncle, he too was one of those who had gone to the city with his family to seek work. He did well and, although not rich like Senhor Sousa, he lives a pleasant life. It was he who took me out of the forest and brought me up as his own. I still see some of those who are left of my family when I take tourists into the forest. I never take them into that village of course.' He added quickly. 'I slip away at night and join them for a short time. These people wish to be left alone. Foreigners have done great damage to such villages and harmed the people in the past Senhor. There are less and less of them now. I think I will make it possible for you to visit them, Senhor Lockwood, because of your father; I have listened to stories about him when I was a boy and I think he was good man. But first I will take you to all of the places he would have seen if that is your wish. Some of them are not on my normal tourist routes. For this to happen, it must be just the two of us without other people. You cannot be part of a tour you understand?' It was a question and a statement. I said of course.

'This will be more expensive and will be much more difficult for you too. It will not be like a tour. There will just be the two of us.' He waited to see if I would object to this. When none came he continued. 'It will not be a one or two-day journey, Senhor Lockwood. There will be extra supplies because of that, and extra fuel. You will be my only fare and you will get all my attention. I shall give you much more information about everything we see.' He smiled. 'I hope to enjoy myself much more than with my usual clients. Some are like children and I have to keep an eye on them for their safety. I am sure you will be like your father and learn quickly.' He had finished his explanation of what was in store for me and looked across at me expectantly for an answer. I could detect no hidden agenda from all he had said. It sounded reasonable. He also sounded more enthusiastic than I would have expected. It was as if I was doing him a favour by going with him. Was I being suckered into a trap? Would this make my worst fears become a reality?

While he had been speaking he had sorted through the pictures and arranged them in a particular order. He passed them back to me.

'Except for a few they are in the order of your father's journey,' he said with a satisfied smile. It was if he was confirming his knowledge and ability, and it was the clincher for me. I needed no further proof that he was telling the truth. José knew what he was talking about. He was the man that good fortune and Philippe Sousa had delivered to me. In any case, I couldn't visualise the latter being part of a scam.

He was no longer a guide and I knew that. He wanted to do this as much as I did. I swallowed hard. Throughout, he had impressed me with his seriousness and no nonsense approach to the task. José Barcelos seemed the answer to my wildest dreams. I was sure no one else could be a better guide to re-live what my father had experienced. My mind went back to that night when he'd first shown me the photos as a boy. Now I could bring them to life and perhaps understand more about the man whom I had always regarded as remote and even stuffy. I was thinking all this even as he spoke. José's concluding sentence about the location of my father's journey brought me back to the present. He was looking apprehensive as if I was about to turn him down. I quickly reassured him.

'I'm sorry, José, I was lost in thought. I was remembering the first time I saw these photographs.' I had a sudden empathy with the man opposite and told him of my upbringing and being unaware of William Lockwood's travels. I poured out my inner thoughts to this stranger whom I had just met for the first time in my life. He listened sympathetically; maybe it was part of his job, maybe not, but I couldn't help myself.

I asked him what it would cost and it was not excessive. I had enquired from Philippe about the cost of such safaris. This was scarcely double that price plus extra expenses for food and fuel for the longer journey. I had my own personal guide and was not part of a group. Even how long it would take us was not discussed. *'When it is over,'* he had said. I felt he wanted to do this for own satisfaction too. *This would not be escorting rich tourists into the rain forests to take pictures of native Indians so that they could show their friends back home. Here was someone with a real interest in his heritage, not looking for trophies on a safari.*

I decided to follow my instincts, and accepted his offer. I held out my hand and he grabbed it with a big smile. It was not a triumphant smile of clinching a contract. It was one of enthusiasm for what he looked forward to. I was no longer a client. I was a friend accompanying him on an adventure.

'From now on, José,' I said, 'I am Martin not Senhor Lockwood, OK?'

I began to ask his advice on clothing and he said he would take me into town the next day and I could purchase them with his help. He knew all the right stores for the best prices and the best quality. He would buy the necessary supplies for the trip at the same time. All this reassured me I was not just a paying customer. I sensed an underlying excitement in his calm exterior and I was in safe hands. It was still only late afternoon and we chatted some more. I ordered a couple of beers. We talked about other things beside the forthcoming trip. I learned about his upbringing with his uncle and the poverty that he saw and still sees. He didn't boast but he was proud of the way he had worked hard to attain a better lifestyle. He was proud of his boat and his independence. Underlying it all I sensed sadness in his voice for the indigenous tribes that had seen their numbers decimated by disease and exploitation from various foreigners over the centuries. He wanted to know about life in Britain, and even though he had read about it at school, my own education bewildered him. It brought home to me how privileged I'd been compared with his own struggles to escape from poverty. When I mentioned the knowledge stored in the Bodleian and the Ashmolean, he was open-mouthed. I had taken it all for granted. I'd never appreciated that they were at my disposal whenever I needed them for information.

As always happens when two men become friends for the first time and become slightly drunk, we eventually ran out of conversation regarding the matter on hand. That was tomorrow and all was taken care of. Then it was family, followed by jobs and education and so on. A couple of beers later and it was as if we were fellow students on our first night out together away from college. Girls were mentioned, quickly followed by conquests of the fair sex. As virtual strangers, there is never anyone to dispute or confirm the facts; we were no exception, José and I. First one and then the other would recall some sexual encounter, starting with the first time each one had had a girlfriend. Eventually licence was added to the anecdotes and we laughed at the other's successes and failures. It was all light-hearted and not toe-curling. Finally I told him about my previous night's escapade. His jaw dropped when I said how much the threesome had cost me. I said the price would not be exceptional in London for such high-class escorts. Although I'd never tried them. His reaction somehow added stature to the episode and helped salve my deflated ego regarding the amount I had parted with. I was definitely warming to my Brazilian guide and newfound confidant. I looked forward to my trip into the unknown with more relish than I thought possible than when I had arrived here. He was no longer a stranger.

We finally ran out of things to brag about and became serious again as it was time for him to get home. He touched briefly on some of the things I would encounter in the next week or two and some of the dangers. He outlined them lightly, perhaps not wishing to discourage me in any way. It was his final attempt to see if I was serious and couldn't be put off. It was a satisfying end to the night and we parted company.

I didn't sleep much that night; there was so much for my brain to take in. There was no backing out now. If I had any misgivings I had to put them all behind me. I'd come all this way on a flight of fancy after seeing my father's effects and I'd been more than lucky in my contacts so far. Fate had treated me kindly, or at least it appeared so. Perhaps it was the enthusiasm of youth. Perhaps my foolhardiness would rebound before it was all over and the rainforest would wreak its revenge for my newfound light-hearted attitude. Would my luck hold? Would I return unscathed as my father did? In the end I gave up and got dressed. I prepared my equipment, at least the few items I had purchased myself for the trip. I packed the rest in the suitcase I had travelled with from England. Even then I had time to spare, so I opened the diary in which I intended to record a daily account of what I would encounter in this unknown future. If I returned unscathed, it would be something for any heir to read, just as I had read my father's. I made my first entry of the day's events. I finished with, 'May the force be with me.' It may be the only time I would be flippant. After breakfast I went outside to wait for the arrival of Senhor Barcelos.

Chapter 7

Promptly at ten o'clock, José arrived in an old Ford Mustang that had seen better days. He discretely parked it away from the front of the hotel, but the blue smoke and noise from a broken exhaust heralded his arrival. I quickly went out to meet him, earning a quizzical look from the receptionist.

The city was unbearably hot when we drove in and other exhaust fumes filled the air. There were quite a few other old cars amongst the shiny new ones belonging to the blossoming economy. Speed seemed essential with all of them and the noise was deafening. Senhor Barcelos knew his way around and I became increasingly pleased with my luck at having him as my guide. Dented bumpers were the norm and it reminded me of some Italian cities. He took me to various suppliers and outfitters. They all knew him of course, and I suppose he benefited from the sales. It was part of his job but I'm sure the items would have been more expensive had I bought them myself. I didn't begrudge him any commission he may have gained. We made a morning of it and he found a suitable café for a snack. It was fish of course; the rivers abound with countless species, as I would find out. I didn't enquire the name of this one. They never tasted the same due to the flair of the different chefs in each establishment, but they always tasted delicious. This was no exception.

He dropped me off afterwards saying it would take him another day to prepare his boat and stow all the essentials aboard. We shook hands warmly as seemed the tradition amongst these people. It was quite unlike the formal handshake in Britain. It was more than hello or goodbye. It was if I was a member of his family and wouldn't see him till next year. I carried the parcels up to my room and couldn't wait to take a second look and try them on.

For the rest of the day and tomorrow, I'd make the most of the modern amenities of the hotel. I had no wish to go into the city again. It would be hang the expense. José had shown me most of the places of interest and parked the Mustang seemingly anywhere for me to take photos. I intended to enjoy the comparative cool rooms of the hotel. Later that evening I took yet another shower and thought I'd try on my new jungle outfit. I stood in front of the mirror and admired Martin Lockwood, the would-be modern-day intrepid explorer. A little different from my father and the other explorers I had seen pictures of. No shorts or helmet, instead a light denim combat suit with a draw-string at the ankles. *To keep out some of the nasties José had informed me of when I purchased them with his approval.* A broad brimmed hat completed the picture and a cotton neckerchief *to soak up the sweat.*

One of our calls had been to a Farmacia where they had made up a small parcel of proprietary brand medicines that were on offer to tourists. I refrained from reading the labels; it was all in Portuguese anyway.

'Anything else we need I can get as we go along. There are enough natural medicines growing in the forest to satisfy most of our needs,' José said. He said it casually and I sensed it was an understatement. He would be on hand to administer should the need arise, he added, and by now I had complete faith in his knowledge.

I set the camera up on the dressing table and took a few snaps of myself while the equipment was in pristine condition. I kidded myself it was the start of my catalogue of photographs to go with my diary and not a sop to my ego. I duly recorded the pictures in my first entry in that diary. I packed all the stuff away and got dressed for dinner. Despite enjoying the luxury of the hotel for all of the following day, I had difficulty suppressing my excitement as I woke on the day I was to meet José and the real journey would begin. Fully kitted out to brave what lay in store I locked the door, shouldered my backpack and picked up my suitcase containing the clothes I'd arrived in. The lift took me down to the ground floor and reception. I paid my hotel bill and handed the suitcase over to the girl behind the desk.

'Perhaps you could find someone who could make use of these clothes. I have no need for them where I am going.' She thanked me and I sat in reception to wait for Barcelos. I optimistically contemplated doing the reverse journey and buying new clothes for my return to England. I even envisaged carrying a new valise packed with the diary and SD cards with hundreds of photos from a successful trip. Perhaps it was a daydream too many.

The wait was unbearable, despite not having to wait long for my companion. On this occasion he roared up to the front of the hotel in a cloud of dust. In no time we were at the landing where his boat was moored. He had described his boat the previous night and now he proudly showed me round it. It was some thirty feet long with a Honda outboard motor that could be swung on board when not in use. It was narrow, to negotiate some of the channels that covered the rainforest. Mostly unnamed, they came and went according to the rainfall, as I was to discover. It was big enough to carry him and up to four tourists. At the back was a covered living area with cooking facilities. Hammocks were available for sleeping. I was to find out the advantage of these over bunk beds. He was obviously proud to own such a craft. He was fairly modest about his knowledge of the rainforest, but as the days passed I became aware that during his years of guiding tourists, he had become highly proficient and there was little he didn't know about the environment and the currents of the rivers we encountered. He spotted eddies from under-water rocks and other dangers. From the moment we set off I could depend on him to point out the interesting things and how to avoid the unsuspecting problems, of which there were many. All this as he steered the craft in the direction he intended taking us. It was reassuring. Even so, there was a note of pride in his achievements, given his own poor beginnings. He passed on his knowledge of the different riverboats.

'The forest people still build dugout canoes in the old tradition and you will see how they do this. There are also *jangadas*, a kind of raft with sails; other boats are made from animal skins. There are many different sorts of dugouts, depending on what is growing in their part of the forest. All are carefully crafted and time is of no importance to the makers. They jealously try to fashion a boat better than their neighbour, yet help each other initially with the felling of the tree and bringing it back to the village. In all things they still manage to survive on what God gives them. Each family strives to live as best it can but the village is one family. The men are as brothers and the women sisters. The children all play together and learn well from their parents. The different tribes, for there are many, have learned to take only what they need for their immediate use. This means that the forest will always replace it for them and is never depleted. The forest is their God, their friend, it is their servant and is part of them. Some of the tribes make a little money making various artefacts, crude pottery and works of art. They sell these to the passing *turista*. It is frowned upon by most, as contact with people from the outside can bring diseases that that can quickly wipe out a whole village. They grow crops of tropical corn (maize), and cassava. Even though I grew up with these people I am still amazed how they survive.' When he spoke about the toughness and the ingenuity of these people I could tell he had a great affinity with them still.

Later when we met them it was obvious they all trusted him and they made us welcome because of that trust. He never betrayed their whereabouts. There was an obvious long-standing bond. They still thought of him as one of them. There were one or two of these tribes that he wouldn't visit with tourists. He mentioned one in particular.

'Some people would like to take trips to the *Yanomami* and other small Indian reserves. This is only possible with proper permission from the authorities. There are two of these. One is called the IBAMA, and they protect the *floresta*. The other is FUNAI and this one is supposed to protect the Indians.' *His look told me that he was sceptical about whose welfare the latter had in mind.* 'Permits to visit these people have to be obtained for each visit. If a tour company say they have permission, they are usually telling lies. In any case, permission is only granted to a few. This is because of...' he shrugged his shoulders again and I got the message: red tape and minor officials with their hand out.

'So you see, Martin, most of these trips are illegal and the tourists could find themselves in very bad trouble. Of course you understand the reason why such visits are *mau* – bad. Lone groups of Indians have no immunity to diseases brought in by these strangers. Even the common cold can kill them easily. It is the same for you. Some of the things that do not bother them in the *selva* – the rainforest – would be very unpleasant to you.' *I would soon find out that this was an understatement, and be amazed of the vast areas still unexplored.*

'The very first invaders gave these people measles, smallpox and other diseases,' he went on. 'This killed lots of the forest dwellers. Others, of course, made slaves of them and forced them to live on their plantations. They mistreated the men and raped their women. You can still see descendents of these children today even in the cities. Some tribes managed to escape and hide deep in the forested areas along the Amazon and the Rio Negro. That is where they have remained to this day. Despite that, they were still not completely out of danger. For two hundred years the Portuguese invaders would carry out Indian-hunting slave raids, from São Paulo and other towns. Whole families would be taken – the men and young boys were worked to death, the women and girls ill-used by the plantation owners. Over the long years of this, many Indian populations blended with European or African people.'

As we talked one-to-one, he could tell I was sympathetic to his cause and my response was genuine. Perhaps my father too had understood.

I could tell that when José explained the plight of these people to his normal boatload of tourists he was pissing in the wind.

The boat was immaculately turned out. Its owner gave me a short tour of inspection and pointed to a seat under the awning; it was to be mine when not otherwise engaged. I settled into it and looked around at what would be my new home for the near future.

José lowered the outboard into the water and did the necessary adjustments to the motor. There was a splutter and then a roar as he fired up the motor. Well cared for, it settled into a quiet 'put-put' and when everything seemed to his satisfaction he cast off. I looked back to the jetty and I felt a rush of blood to my heart.

Chapter 8

Gradually the noises of the city receded and I wondered what I would experience before I heard them again. I knew it wouldn't all be plain sailing but I enjoyed those first few moments as we set off. Yet even before the taxi horns and ships' sirens faded, I began to pick up the sounds that replaced them. These would be the ones I would be hearing from now on. It was a sound that was new to me and far removed from what lay beneath the glistening domes of the Eden Project. First it was the birds screeching from the treetops and then animal sounds, mostly monkeys. They were a long way off and when we finally reached the rainforest proper the noise would exceed the decibels of the city. At least I thought so, but perhaps I was more used to those.

As we sat gliding serenely along with the rhythmic put-put of the motor – a most pleasant experience – I stole a glance at my guide now that he was in his work attire. There was little noticeable difference except he now had an air of authority. He was now the man in charge. He was the tourist guide who knew all the answers. He had shut out the city by thought and deed and belonged to where we were going. These thoughts were not derogatory and I didn't feel superior. It was a statement of fact. I was now an ignorant stranger subservient to him and his people. He was the expert.

The responsibility hardly showing on his face, José Barcelos looked relaxed. There was no slightly furrowed brow that was discernable during our first meeting. It had been a business meeting and he was endeavouring to negotiate a contract. Now he was at home in familiar surroundings. Despite the noise of the forest creatures, the river was fairly benign in comparison to what I had expected. It was huge of course, but the sky was blue and, although it was hot, there was a cool breeze. Apart from the noise, I could have been floating in a punt on a lazy Saturday afternoon on the Thames. It was all a false impression of what lay ahead, a ploy on the part of the elements to lure me into their clutches. I took advantage of it. Beneath my new outfit I could smell talc and aftershave. It would be a long time before I smelled like that again.

Jose's voice broke into my reverie, telling me of our first destination, a place called Aiparuca, about forty miles northwest. This he said was usually on one of his short tours during which he would take the party there and back in a day. They would have lunch in the town there and buy their souvenirs. In between he would point out the wildlife on the banks and in the trees and they snapped away with their cameras. When they returned home after their holiday they knew all about the rainforest and its people. There was a slight amused expression when he said this. It was obvious from our short time together in Manaus; he knew I was not that type of client. After all we did get slightly drunk and disclose our inner thoughts.

'It is what they expect of me, Martin. I point out the places and the animals and birds and they are satisfied. It is a good arrangement, everybody is happy. Of course they could learn all this, I tell them, and more in an encyclopaedia, or on Google,' he laughed. 'They could visit the Jungle Park in Manaus, but that would be cheating.' He laughed again. 'With hand on heart they can swear they have endured the real thing.' His next remark was of no consolation to me. The glint in his eye showed it was said purposely for his own amusement and to make me prepared for the worst.

'They never experience the real hardship that you will, Martin. They never get close to the action. There is little danger from their adventure. Most of them are from the USA and Japan and their cameras never stop clicking. When they get home they will be the envy of all their friends. Still, it is one of my most popular excursions. There are longer tours in other directions.

With you of course it will be different. You have a purpose. As this is a long journey we will spend more time exploring and I will go into more detail. We shall get closer to the wildlife. At our first stop, as I said, it will be Aiparuca. But we will not seek the luxury of the town. We will sleep in the boat on the river near to the forest. It is better you get used to the harshness straight away. This will be as your father travelled and what you would wish, não?' I had little choice it seemed; I'd burned my bridges and he was piling on the agony of what lay in store.

That first day with José made the greatest impact on my life up till then. This was the Eden Project on a grand scale. There were no protective domes to shelter from the elements.

Everything was untamed. The river widened out till it was ten miles across in places, due to the constant flooding of tropical rainstorms. These were a common feature throughout the rainforests, I would learn.

José landed at various places during the day for half an hour or so. He wanted me to get used to the forest gradually for the latter part of our journey. It was a good opportunity also he said, to capture pictures on my camera, as we would be close up to the wildlife. He would jump ashore and I would toss him the rope to tie up. We swapped roles later. More and more we became a team as the days went by. I felt less and less like a tourist. As we landed it appeared to be normal riverside vegetation. A few yards in and it changed to tall, overhead canopies that blotted out the sky.

The trees were festooned with trailing ivies and parasitic plants all seeking sustenance as they attached themselves to their host. They grew at a fantastic speed. I had seen TV programmes of time-lapse sequences where plants appeared to snake out into the air. I'm sure if I stood still and watched for half an hour it would happen before my eyes.

Very little sunlight penetrated and the humidity took away my breath. Nothing lay unattended for long. If anything dropped from the canopy it was devoured or used by some creature. The forest floor moved as ants and other insects tried to keep up with the debris that fell to earth. I had read that eight thousand species of insects have been identified and I can believe it. Most of them were welcoming me in their own unpleasant way. They sought out every orifice for their own particular food and drink. There were scores of different mosquitoes and I only hoped my injections were effective against them. Mosquitoes of course were what one expected. They are the scourge of hot countries and something every schoolboy reads about. But I soon discovered another flying menace that was even worse. These were tiny black flies, namely Piums, and they bit every exposed bit of flesh. Though insignificant in size, the red spots from their bites itched for days afterwards. I constantly had to knock ticks and bugs off my clothing. Everything I saw was larger than life.

In contrast were the thousands of butterflies in every colour of the rainbow. They hovered over the riverbanks in clouds, procreating and laying down another million eggs. Birds and other predators fed on them and their offspring, apparently without diminishing their numbers. Fireflies glowed eerily as dusk began to fall, their lights moving about like twinkling stars. The sight of them and the butterflies compensated a little for their relatives during the day. On that first day José pointed out bees, wasps and hornets as noisy and as large as small helicopters. They zoomed past oblivious of my nervousness and were of little danger unless aggravated by a bad day at the office. Amongst the ground leaves were scorpions, centipedes and cockroaches, large enough to crunch underfoot and good enough to eat, said Jose. I'll take his word for it, but hope I never need to. Giant spiders abseiled down trees as we passed. It was all very unnerving and I think my guide got a bit of a kick out of it, as he did with all his tourists. At the end of that first day I learned to grit my teeth if I felt something crawling on the back of my neck. I would casually ask José to remove it rather than swat at it, just in case. Sweat tickled and dribbled all over and this was unnerving. I didn't know if it was sweat or a creepy-crawly. There's a saying: what can't be cured must be endured and my nerve endings finally stopped warning me. Continually there was the off-key squawk of toucans high in the trees as we came within range, but I only caught glimpses of them through the canopy. Parrots and macaws were easy to see. Twice a day they screeched, waking us at dawn like an alarm clock and then last thing at night, making it difficult for me to sleep. José had no such problem. I did eventually get used to it, after a fashion. It's like living near a railway station I suppose. Howler monkeys joined in on these occasions. Squirrel monkeys were numerous but I had to take José's word for it. They were smaller and it was virtually impossible to get them on camera. I pointed the camera in their direction and hoped when I edited them back home something would appear on zoom. It was a good initiation on that first day and I had learned a lot from José, and my own observation, on those shore excursions. I certainly knew what I was letting myself in for if I was to survive.

We saw a smoky haze in the distance, showing that we had reached the outskirts of Aiparuca. With his years of experience, my guide found a suitable inlet away from the main river, which had a low count of insects. He said that in this particular area all the trees were covered with a large growth of a climbing plant that deterred most insects. He didn't know what it was called and hadn't attempted to find out. I suggested he should approach a pharmaceutical company with that knowledge.

'It would probably make someone a fortune as an insect repellent,' I said.

'I know that, but the forest would be torn down to process it. I think I'll keep the place secret for my own use when I pass this way.'

For some reason it seemed cooler here than any place we'd seen all day. Perhaps because of the lack of insects, the whole food chain gave the place a wide berth.

He tied the boat up and lowered a net canopy to protect us from any intrepid insect that could be scouting in the area. He had already pointed out various fish that were in abundance throughout the journey, and asked if I would like to try my hand at catching one. I jumped at the chance. My notebook was filled with facts about the flora and fauna of the environments surrounding us so I already knew there were countless species of fish. He handed me a reel of nylon with a hook at the end. There was no need for a rod, he said. He poked under some leaves and picked up a grub of some sort.

'There is plenty of these about,' he said, 'any sort will catch a fish.' He stuck it on the hook at the end of the line and handed it to me. I simply threw the line over the side of the boat and undid the reel. In no time at all there was a fish on the end of the line. It was a catfish and, being here, the size of its namesake. He chopped off the head and tail with a machete and threw them over the side. It was all done so quickly I think it was still alive as he gutted it. In that climate you don't mess about with the niceties of preparation, or you could be sharing it with some sharp-eyed passing predator from above and lose a finger in the process, he informed me. He got rid of the innards in the same way, swilling it in the water; quickly I noted. He placed the fish in a pan on the fire he had lit while I had been catching it. There was a sprinkling of oil in the bottom and it started sizzling. As he did so the water churned at the side of the boat. I looked over and saw the discarded parts of the catfish disappearing before my eyes. I noticed during the day that there was very little rubbish lying around in the forest. Everything was consumed by something. The food chain was a complete circle. The piranhas or some other shoal of hungry fish had their tea before we did. As José finished cooking the fish, I meticulously searched the cabin for unwanted nasties and destroyed them before we sat down. 'You will make someone a good housewife,' he said.

It was a simple meal of grilled fish and rough bread followed by black coffee. José poured out two glasses of liquid from a bottle with no label. It tasted a little like brandy but who knows. My breath would certainly take care of any small insect remaining under the netting. José lit a foul-smelling cigar and, although I don't smoke, I was pleased; I think it destroyed any remaining insects. I looked through the photos that I had taken so far on the small camera screen. Once more I appreciated how easy it was to take and store them in the memory cards. Without such modern facilities, my father would have had to store rolls of film till he returned home, in the hope that he had some successes. After today's experience I can only imagine how much of a hit and miss affair that would be. I doubt if he would have had a guide like José and it was unlikely the fellow could speak English. His nights must have been lonely and traumatic. I was very lucky to have José. The man in question had finished his cigar and looked across at me. The clearing was an oasis. It had a spring at one end and I cleaned up the tin plates and returned to the boat. My chores were finished and we were both free to talk.

We talked about the day's events and I expressed my satisfaction at what I had seen and the photos. He traced our journey on the map and indicated tomorrow's route. I felt more a companion than a paying tourist. I asked him more about the Indian tribes that were scattered over the rainforests. I knew it was a subject close to his heart. My questions weren't patronising and he knew it. I was genuinely interested in their way of life and as we would meet them eventually if all went well, I wanted to be prepared. He gave me a background on their history. It was from his point of view and not what I would research from books.

He said that in 1988, over three hundred Indian communities were given their own territories. 'Of course it was theirs in the first place,' he added. 'They had lived here thousands of years before they were invaded. Some of these reservations cover thousands of square miles. The total area is more than one-tenth the area of Brazil. It was a way of getting rid of the indigenous people. Most of the land was thought to be only good enough for such people. Unfortunately, some Brazilians do not always respect these reservations. *Garimpeiros* have trespassed in several of these reserves and violence has broken out.'

I asked who these *Garimpeiros* were and he said they were miners who travelled about looking for work. A kind of gypsy workforce of stateless people he supposed, living on whatever they came across, irrespective of whom it belonged to. His remarks were biased because of his background but I couldn't deny his logic. His people had been denigrated in the eyes of their conquerors into second-class citizens. It had been their land and had had it taken away from them.

Even though we were in a quiet backwater, the noises all around still made me uneasy. This clearing that José had picked out for us was a virtual Shangri-La compared to what we would have to undergo in the main. But, I could still detect noises all around and disturbances in the water too, and I thought I'd never sleep. My Portuguese guide sensed this and handed me another, even larger measure of the unknown spirit and before long I climbed into my hammock, a popular item in this part of the world for obvious reasons. It's less accessible to the wildlife than a bed. The day had exhausted me and the noises around seemed to lessen. The toucans and the howler monkeys seem to have made up their differences and their screeching had diminished. Perhaps José's concoction had something to do with it. Whatever the reason I slept soundly, but not surprisingly after all I'd seen on that first day, I had dreams. Perhaps it was the firewater, maybe the heavy meal of fish, but some of the images were nightmarish.

A steamy mist surrounded the bottom half of the boat and pencil-thin shafts of light moved across under its canvas roof. The screechers were tuning up and in a split second I knew I wasn't in the Eden Project. The shadow of the tall Portuguese moved across me and the smell of coffee slowly stirred my brain into activity. I opened my eyes and recalled yesterday's events. Apart from the innumerable and differently shaped red spots that covered my body I appeared to be healthy enough. I had a slight hangover but my appetite was OK. Breakfast was a hunk of the same coarse bread and fruit that we had picked up on our travels the previous day. José took it from a sealed container hung from the canopy of the boat to prevent it attracting insects or decaying in the humid atmosphere. I soon

111

learned that nothing could be left exposed for long before a creature with finely tuned olfactory senses detected it and carried it off. Alternatively, an army of giant ants honed in on it and it disappeared as you watched.

I carried out my crude ablutions as quickly as possible, cleansing all orifices diligently. These were a special target, said José. He showed me certain items from my medicine chest that would help to deter some of the more persistent insects from targeting these. There was also an ointment for soothing the ones I already had.

I used fresh rainwater where it had collected in the large leaves to clean my teeth. He advised me not to use the spring water.

'It may look clean and feel fresh and cool, but it gets polluted even as it bubbles from the ground. It is OK for washing up the cooking pans. I always put plenty of spices in the food.'

I followed suit when he splashed some of it over his head. I certainly felt better for it. I had full confidence in my new friend; for that's what he was. He didn't feel like a guide any more. He was my teacher, my mentor, and I could rely on him. He had evolved a lifestyle from his background and his city life that was the best of both worlds. He had selected all the good things from each. He was a wise man.

We were just about to cast off when he pointed upward with his finger and motioned me to keep still. High above, a hawk was hovering over the clearing. I couldn't identify it. It was impossible to distinguish colour or even size. It was just a silhouette. The clearing was ideal for it and José told me later he had watched it on other occasions. It remained motionless for a minute or so and then swooped down in a steep dive from one end to the other. Its target was a small mammal drinking at the spring. It was most likely a small rat or a mouse. The hawk picked it up cleanly from ground and made off, landing on the nearest tall tree. Holding it firmly with its claws, it killed it with one small peck. It then flew off with its prize. Hawks in Britain do the same thing of course, but the opportunity to see it happen is rare and usually confined to TV programmes.

The sun had already started to burn off the low, overnight mists and I looked forward to seeing new sights on day two. I felt completely at home with José. His conversation was mostly confined to explaining the animals, fish, reptiles and birds that were constantly making appearances. When we stopped for food, however, we would share personal details about each other. His life had been simple, he said, but he was eager to know about what England was like. He had the impression that the population was so huge that people were stepping on each other's toes. I told him about the beautiful countryside and the temperate climate.

'It may not be as big as Brazil, but you can walk around with little fear of being frozen, burned or eaten alive by animals, birds or insects.'

I described the Lake District and the Yorkshire moors. I explained the diversity of each season.

'Wherever you live you're no more than seventy-five miles from the sea.' It was one of the facts that had him bemused. University life had him open-mouthed. My private life amongst girl students had him envious. I could see that and I tried hard not to gild the lily. To sum up, we became educated in our different environments because of our daily contact without the distraction of tutors or other students.

Surrounded by wildlife we were the only two people in the world, depending on each other. Although he was the guide with all the knowledge of his familiar surroundings I felt I was contributing to the team. I carried out the various chores he asked me to do as we progressed. He trusted me more than any of his normal tourists. I was no longer a stranger in his eyes. We were two men exploring together and enjoying each other's company. I felt privileged.

Before we rejoined the main river where we had turned off the previous night I saw the giant water lilies I'd missed in the darkness the night before. These huge, majestic floating plants are mainly found in fully lit quieter backwaters of the muddy river flood plains. The giant saucer-shaped leaves can reach nearly two yards in diameter. The large white flowers were as big as footballs. The size of some of the plant life still leaves me shaking my head. The ones in the Eden Project were never this big. José explained that as the water level drops, the lily pads and their stems are left on dry ground and become decomposed. The roots however, remain alive and new stems sprout with the next floods. The stems can grow several centimetres each day to keep up with the rising water levels, sometimes up to five metres. Several species of marsh birds, similar to coots and water hens but different in colour, had nests on the lilies. Theirs was a precarious life-style. They were attacked by birds of prey from above and were constantly on the alert. They would frequently dive overboard to avoid these aerial predators. Then they risked the under-water dangers of snakes and other predators – I knew there were alligators but so far hadn't seen any. José said they basked in the sun on the banks and attacked anything there or in the water. I was constantly in awe of my surroundings and told him so.

'It's like Jurassic Park,' I said and told him about the film. He was equally amazed at Britain, its small size and large population.

We covered about fifty miles on the second day and it lasted from dawn till dusk. The riverbed had widened out even more. Flocks of parakeets were always flying overhead. It was said that there were more of these than sparrows in the USA and I could believe it. Because of the time of the year, the water was fairly low. This wide section was known as the *Arquipélago das Anavilhana*. Several islands had been formed over the centuries with silt from the mountains and these were quite visible. Now and again José would point out places as we passed and show me where they were on my father's photos. He handed one to me now.

'See Martin, your father came in the winter and the islands are almost under water. Our next overnight stay will be opposite the town of Santo Antonio. This is on the other bank and at the end of the Arquipélago, and here the Rio Negro narrows slightly; this is because it divides into two and then rejoins itself later.'

A large island had been formed by this phenomenon and José steered the boat over towards this raised land and moored up. It was a detour away from the direction of Santo Antonio, our eventual destination, but he wanted me to see it. He jumped out and beckoned me to follow.

'We will spend a little time here,' he said. 'Even I am amazed at what has happened because of this new island.'

Our stay there would also be for my benefit too, I knew that. He always thought of what was best for me. We set out to explore the wonders of this central reservation. It had become a zoo in its own right. Around the edges were herons spaced out, each with their own territory. A flock of roseate spoonbills rose as we neared them and settled down behind us as we passed, almost unafraid. José said it was a little world of its own with every animal, bird and insect to complete a food chain.

'In a year or maybe ten, it will become flooded again and they will all disappear.' I added to his conjecture as I kicked the soil underfoot.

'This soil is full of goodness from the mountains. I think it will create new species of plants and insects in time, José.' I had told him about the Eden Project. 'A botanist from there would die for the opportunity to study here.' This was a hands-on horticultural lesson and I would never get bored.

Because of this cycle of flooding there were no large trees. While we were there, the sun shone and the rain held off. We left this paradise and made our way back downstream. I was ecstatic and couldn't stop talking about the wonders of what we had seen. My enthusiasm rubbed off on José, too. His years of travelling through the rainforests had made him blasé, but he admitted later how lucky he was to see these natural wonders for nothing. He had made this detour just to show me those wonderful sights and I not only enjoyed the visit tremendously, I felt very privileged.

Eventually, we resumed our intended direction and made towards the eastern arm of the Rio Negro. The smoke from Santo Antonio told us we had arrived at our stopping place for the night. It was several miles away but José, as usual, didn't intend that we should be disturbed. José turned the craft into a tributary and then into an even smaller one till he felt sure we wouldn't be discovered by a stray tourist trip.

Once again, he found a haven, if there are such places in Amazonas; not by accident I guessed. It was a clearing, but this time people had created it, probably illegal tree poachers from Santo Antonio, he said. It had once been a standing of walnut trees. To make it worse, rubbish had been left, the sort that would not disappear naturally such as plastic bags, oil and chemical drums. A large area of deforestation had taken place and unwanted trees had been left to rot. Whether legal or not, José couldn't tell but I was glad of it. There would be less likelihood of danger during the night than on the boat. We secured it and covered it with bushes. I helped him set up camp well away from the riverbank. I was accustomed to what was needed now and did it with relish. I began to feel more like a guide than a tourist every day. He noticed this and remarked upon it.

'Maybe you should stay and work for me when we return to Manaus,' and he laughed in his usual friendly way. It was said tongue in cheek but he knew my sense of humour by now. I replied in a similar vein.

'You couldn't afford to pay me enough,' I replied, 'and I like the pleasures of the city too much.'

As usual he did most of the work so I always volunteered to catch fish and other menial tasks that were within my scope. I liked that. He showed me the most likely place, and the safest, he added.

'I don't think there are any piranhas at this spot, but if you are not sure, kill them before taking them off the line. I would not like one of your *dedos* for supper.' I think he was pulling my leg but I followed his instructions very carefully. He left me to it. I caught quite an assortment by the time he shouted he was ready to cook them. I felt rather pleased. He discarded a few saying they were inedible, the rest we shared. I don't think I've ever enjoyed fish as much at home as I did there. Catching it yourself is a real thrill as you eat it. You know it's fresh. He smoked his cigar and measured out the usual two large nightcaps again. We talked about what we'd seen during the day and he added one of the folklore anecdotes that had come his way over the years. This one was particularly fascinating. He was reminded of it as he threw away the unwanted fish.

'There is a very tiny fish almost as thin as thread,' he said. 'It is attracted by blood in the water after a piranha kill. I've been told it can enter a woman as she stands in the water washing clothes especially if she has woman trouble. It then enters her stomach and she will die; that I believe. However, there are stories of it entering a man as he pisses in the water. But I have never met any of these men so perhaps it is a story to keep children away from the dangers of the river.' *True or not, I don't think I'll risk any part of my anatomy in these waters.*

It was during this conversation that I discovered something that had not occurred to me before. I mentioned that I had not seen any of my dad's photos of the boat that had taken him on his journey.

'That is because I don't think he would have had one,' was his simple reply. The statement staggered me.

'You mean he made the journey on foot, through the forest?' I replied. He nodded. I was silent for a moment.

'Then his journey must have been even more arduous than mine,' I said in awe. José nodded once more.

'He would have probably had two or more local men to carry all his equipment and supplies. He would have to set up camp every night in the forest. It would be a hard journey. He would have maps and a compass of course, but he would depend on his bearers to know about local dangers as they went. It would be unlikely they could speak English so it was a silent journey for him. I could see he too was in awe of my father. I never spoke throughout the meal and I think he knew why. I was trying to digest what he had told me. My father's stature was growing day by day, and my attempt to emulate him paled in comparison, notwithstanding the good fortune I had experienced since arriving in Brazil. He had successfully fulfilled his ambition and returned home with his journal complete and the black and white stills as proof. He had taken up a sedentary life as a barrister and apparently never bragged about his exploits. Whatever I did would not compare in terms of effort and single-mindedness. All my life I had thought of him as a stuffy and boring old lawyer. As I learned more about his practically sole effort, my own seemed to lessen in comparison. I'd had the services of José, a friendly English-speaking experienced guide and was treated as an equal. He had nursed me through when I was green, with his know-how without making me feel like a burden. I had been very lucky. When, and if I get through, I will be more modest in my account if I relate it to friends at the Eden Project. And I shall certainly tell them the extent of what William Lockwood went through forty years ago.

It was the third day on the river and today we were making for Novo Airão – another forty miles or so. Each day there are new animals and fish to see. José would sometimes go close to the banks deliberately to disturb anacondas, boa constrictors and lizards of every shape and size. I am still amazed by the size of some of these creatures close up. On television I never felt the menace of them. I saw what I thought was a lizard in the distantce, only to be told it was an iguana. When we drew near, it was three feet long. José said some of them grow to two metres. It was basking in the sun on the bank and we passed quite close to it. One eye opened and closed lethargically. Insects ran across it as if it were a rock. It ignored them. The boa constrictors were green above and yellow underneath and as long as ten to twelve feet. I have always enjoyed nature programmes on TV and been impressed by the presenter's proximity to the wildlife. Now I was scared stiff a safe distance away. The large snakes would sometimes slide away as we approached them. There were turtles and fresh-water dolphins in the deeper water and the river teemed with fish. He spoke of the manatees but I only caught a glimpse of one. It quickly disappeared into the murky depths where they spend most of their time grazing off the bottom. My camera clicked away and I visualised editing them all back in Cornwall. I had read that there were jaguars, tapirs, red deer, and capybara – a large rodent – but so far had only caught glimpses of the many monkeys and what could have been a deer. I mentioned this to José.

'Tomorrow we will turn off the Rio Negro and follow the Rio Jau deep into the rainforest. The wilder animals you talk about are more likely to be deep in the forest; they avoid the riverbanks. After a few more miles I will take you down a very narrow stream that very few people know about. Then we tie the boat up and go on foot through the forest to our destination. You will see more of the forest animals there.' He smiled after this last remark. I began to sense an undercurrent of happiness in his manner as we progressed. It was if he was getting far more out of this tour than previous ones. He enjoyed our relationship because of my keenness. I was obviously different from his usual clients. They would treat him as a paid guide doing his job at their bidding.

On the other hand, I began to think things would get worse for me. Perhaps I hoped not to see the jaguar and his friends after all. About midday he pulled into one of the many tributaries for a rest. Of course it was one he picked out especially for its safety and as usual it had a clearing. The mosquitoes were less in evidence and the ticks seem to realise I had become immune from their efforts. This was mainly due to José's administrations and potions. He pointed out a tiny fresh water rivulet bubbling over some rocks. It must have been from an underground spring. The water was cold and clear and this time safe to drink, he said. I stripped off without even asking if it was safe to do so. I kept on my underpants to be on the safe side. I preferred not to be bitten in that region. I stank of sweat and washed my clothes and myself. José took the hint, but all he did was pour buckets of water over his body. I arranged my clothes on the canopy of the boat to dry. We stayed an hour and had lunch. José picked out another variety of fish from my catch. Although our diet never varied much (it was fish, fruit and bread) José seemed to give the fish a different taste every day and we never seemed to eat the same fish. It was a rough but satisfying diet and far tastier than frozen stuff from a supermarket.

I enquired if he was a vegetarian as we never ate meat and the forest seemed to be full with all kinds of animals. He said it was a lot more trouble than getting fish.

'Large animals are too much for the two of us to eat,' he said, 'and we can't keep the rest fresh, for you know what would happen to it in this heat. Scavengers would soon surround us. I have never considered attempting to catch small animals with my tours. Some of the small animals could carry infections and it would be too risky. I wouldn't want one of my clients to die. If I go alone deep into the forest I trap certain ones and cook them. The forest people have no such worries. But they only kill enough for their needs and that is what I do. They have learned to keep a balance with their surroundings; it is a pity the rest of the people in the world do not do the same. When we abandon the boat and go on foot, we will eat meat.'

When it was time to resume our journey, my clothes were ready to put on – freshly laundered but well creased. I felt better than I had done since I'd left the hotel. Unfortunately the feeling didn't last long; I was soon sweating again.

This is our fourth day on the river, but this will be different, I know. Last night as we enjoyed our usual after-dinner drink and José puffed away his smoke at the mosquitoes, he had gone into detail about today.

'It will be quite different to what you have become used to.' He spoke more seriously than I'd heard him before.

'Most of tomorrow's journey will be on foot through the forest. It will be similar to the way your father travelled. The rainforest quickly becomes overgrown in just a few weeks after cutting a path through it and even though I have travelled these ways before it always looks different. Trees will have fallen and floodwater will have washed away paths. We will have to cut fresh paths as we go. There will be several miles of this before we enter the deep part of the forest to the place where the tribe of my family live. There are only about fifty members living in this village and they are called the Nucutani people. These are the ones where I was born and lived before I went to live in Manaus with my uncle; my mother was his sister. They are friendly people and will be pleased to see the son of the man who came here all those years ago.'

I suddenly felt privileged. He was taking me to meet his family, something I'm sure he'd never done with any of his other tourists' excursions. This was the tribe my father had visited, and respected their privacy by keeping a secret of their whereabouts. It dawned on me how fate had brought us together for this reunion. José had realised that when I'd first met him and told him my story. He must have been eager to bring me here and look after my well-being. It's also why he trusted me now. I felt very proud of my father at that moment but very sad; I never really knew him. Why could he never tell me about this amazing land? I'm sure I would have been as enthusiastic as he about it. Were there other reasons that he wouldn't relate the sights I am experiencing now? My mind came back to reality.

I was now approaching the culmination of my travels to Brazil and would be entering the rainforest properly. I could barely suppress my excitement. José's glances towards me told me he guessed about my anticipation and what it meant. There also seemed an air of satisfaction that we had successfully travelled this far without a mishap.

We passed the morning in silence, he I suppose, hoping I would come up to his expectations and that we would reach our final destination without some unseen hazard putting an end to it all. I was determined not to let him down if possible. Both of us were deep in our own thoughts. We'd set off earlier than usual that morning, José saying it was necessary if we intended reaching his people before nightfall. He didn't have to spell out why. Even with his experience of the forest, he didn't want us to be cutting a way through it at night.

Before we had set off he had given me various potions to swallow, none of them proprietary brands. I smeared a foul-smelling ointment on all my exposed flesh and felt some comfort from these precautions. Everything went as he had said. We turned off left into the Rio Jau even as the sun was starting to rise and, after a mile or so, he switched off the engine and we paddled along the bank slowly. Finally he found what he was looking for. It was the opening to a narrow channel, overgrown even since his last visit, he said. He handed me one of a pair of very sharp machetes with eighteen-inch blades.

'You had better practice with it now, Martin; you will be using it quite a lot before the day is out.' He showed me how to bend the thick stems sideways with my left hand and then slash downwards with knife through the bottom of it towards the ground. He handed me a thick, leather, left-handed gauntlet that that also covered my bare wrist for the purpose. He didn't have to explain why this was necessary, and I soon found out what the newly disturbed undergrowth revealed. He stressed that I must stand away from the base of the plant as I did this.

'First it means you won't accidentally cut your foot off and secondly some creature may hiding there and scurry out. As they are not all friendly, you will be ready to use the knife for its second purpose: in your defence. It was a salutary remark and it certainly made me very aware what was round the corner, or under foot in this case. It was remarkable how he found this entrance he was looking for: such is the rapid growth of the greenery in the rainforests. We cleared the entrance to the narrow waterway and we inched along carefully into it. The early morning sun disappeared as we entered the canopy of the forest. I couldn't believe the sudden change after the open river. From the viewpoint of the boat it had never looked this dark. The humidity was stifling. The undergrowth seemed to claw at the boat as it passed through. Left undisturbed since his last visit, clouds of insects rose up, angry at our intrusion. Small animals and reptiles scattered in all directions as if warning their comrades of our coming. They normally would remain undisturbed. Few of them would attack us deliberately, he said.

'Even the snakes will try to avoid us, unless they are hungry,' he added, smiling. I got the picture.

There was a metal frame at the front of the boat with a canvas cover creating extra shelter for the passengers. I used the upright on the right to steady myself as I hacked away at the thick growth on that side. José did the same on the left. We would cut a little and then paddle a little. It was slow progress, but after twenty yards or so, the undergrowth cleared and the channel became clear and widened. I heard the motor start and we continued slowly for a mile or two.

José stared over to the left bank until he saw what he was looking for, stopped paddling, and the craft glided into the side. He had found what he had been looking for. He motioned and we jumped onto the bank. This was another small inlet just a few yards long and a dead end. It was overgrown with lianas. Once more we removed this latest barrier to our progress and pushed the boat into it. Wherever these people were, it seemed impossible for anyone to find them. We filled our two backpacks ready for the journey on foot. José unrolled a tarpaulin and with my help, spread it over the supplies in the bottom of the boat. Finally we covered the canopy of the boat with some of the lianas. The boat was now completely hidden, although I didn't think there'd be many passing tour boats to see it or pirates to hijack it. He gave it a final check. It was his livelihood and his life. He hated leaving it unattended. Without another word, he headed off into the undergrowth with machete raised. I followed suit.

Chapter 9

According to my research, the Amazonian rainforest contains 250 tree species. Before long I saw quite a large number of them. A few I'd seen at the Eden Project. My wonderment there was overshadowed by what I witnessed now. I stared up at giant rubber and the Brazil nut trees that were in abundance. By natural selection they had evolved from their stereotypes to develop bulbous bases called buttresses to prevent being blown down by storms. I spotted rosewood, mahogany and cedar and other very rare specimens. There were countless laurels, palms and acacia. The tallest trees are sun-loving and form a high closed canopy layer overhead, below which there are several lower ones – very little of the sun's rays managed to reach the ground below. As a result, more plants and animals are found in the upper tree branches than on the ground. The high canopy is over a hundred feet high. Through this grow tall, thin white trees seeking the light. These are called emergents and grow another fifty feet or more, reaching into the sky for their existence. Their trunks are covered in lichens and fungus. Most of the trees are covered with a variety of lianas and parasitic climbers that depend on air roots and their host for nutrients. Another unique sight was the sight of flowers growing on the trunks of trees to assist in their pollination. Nature is so innovative and more so here. I saw strange sights of nature that I'd never seen in Britain, and never read about at University.

I soon spotted the animal life, most of it up above where the sun shines. These include insects, snakes, tree frogs, several types of monkeys, and an amazing variety of birds. I am constantly making use of my binoculars as I hear sounds or see movements above me. To begin with it's a bit scary to a town dweller like me. I expect every rustle to be some attacking beast. It takes me quite a while to lose this nervousness. As we went deeper into this jungle the noise became deafening. These creatures were oblivious to our progress and knew they were safe, yet thousands of years have given them this automatic alarm system that they share with their neighbours – friend or foe. It still doesn't prevent a few of them being taken unawares by the few remaining tribes, armed with blowpipes or bows and arrows. As José said, their numbers wouldn't be diminished sufficiently to make them become endangered. It was the outside world that would be responsible for that as they greedily cleared the forests of timber.

Now and again we would pause for a breather, and twice we stopped for food. Some of the trees had drip-tip leaves to shed the rainwater. It was easy to quench our thirst when we stopped. These were the only times when I could really observe all the wonders I've described. I couldn't take my eyes off the job in hand for fear of losing some part of my anatomy. José would point things out and I would ask questions. We would sit on a fallen tree and whisper our questions and answers. In the silence, many of the ground inhabitants would return to the immediate vicinity as if danger to them had passed. José would put a finger to his lips and signal for me to follow him silently. Then he would point through a gap and I would see a deer or a tapir or some of the rodents that inhabit the undergrowth. The jaguar seemed to allude us, or thankfully, perhaps the other way round. Monkeys screamed at us for invading their territory. Some of them spend their entire lives in the canopy. They are safe from most of the predators and food is plentiful. The birds, of course, flew above and below the canopy, squawking and screeching past us. This was unnerving to say the least. Most of them were macaws and parrots of all sizes and colours. This was a zoo beyond the wildest imagination but with no time to study it. My camera never stopped clicking though. I only hope I can manage take the images home safely. It will be wonderful to load them into my computer and show friends. I was exhausted by my efforts towards the end of the morning and as limp as the proverbial wet rag.

What seemed an eternity actually lasted three hours until José found what he was looking for, an opening in the darkness of the canopy. We emerged into a large clearing where the trees had been cut down by human hand. I blinked at the sun. It was still not yet midday. Was this the end of my quest? If so, my ordeal had been worth it. I had experienced an encyclopaedia of flora and fauna in 3D with all the sounds and smells that no book or software could match. As for my own personal body odours, they were lost in the fetid smell of rotting wood and decaying flowers and greenery all around.

At the far end of the clearing was a path and we made for it. We walked on another mile down this path. It was well worn and my excitement grew. Suddenly my guide halted.

'We are now just outside the reserve set apart for what my usual clients and the guidebooks call the Amerindians. This is an area called Terra Indigena Waimiri Atroari. There are many of these reserves in Brazil. This one I think is the largest. It measures one hundred by one hundred and fifty kilometres. It sounds like an enormous gift to these people. In the USA the government gave the Native Americans vast areas of plains. It seemed generous but was of little use for them to make a living from. The buffalo had been wiped out and nothing much grew there. They call them Native Americans now, a polite term for what were called Red Indians.' He said it a little cynically with good reason. I remember the cowboy films when I was young. The Indians would attack forts and encircle settlements and had to be wiped out.

'The reason is the same here,' he went on. 'It keeps *these people* away from the cities.' He emphasised it as if they were looked on as lepers. 'I could tell that most of my American customers thought these tribes in the reservation were similar to their own and were for watching from afar like animals in a zoo. They too, live in reserves.'

There was still a slight bitterness in his voice as he finished. It was an attitude he wouldn't have used on his normal tourist journeys. By now José could speak his mind to me because of our closeness. I think he had detected my sympathy for these indigenous people from the start. Now he could get all his thoughts out of his spleen and there was no need for me to comment. He knew my opinions by now on such subjects. I nodded and told him about Britain's history in that respect.

'Our empire was built on subjecting natives for its financial gain. It was what made Britain rich and powerful. We weren't the only ones. France, Germany, Spain and Portugal, they all did the same. It was something to be proud of, we were told at school. My insular upbringing had made me pay lip service to such enterprise, as it was called. When we read the history books, it was obvious that empire building meant a price was paid by the conquered; dating right back to the Greeks and Romans.'

Senhor José Barcelos was a proud man and had done well for himself from his humble beginnings. He would never want to disassociate himself from his background. He still had a great love for the forest people, and hated to see them demeaned. I was to see more of this respect in the next few days. We never broached the subject again; there was no need.

'The tribe I am taking you to meet are the ones your father found. They are not quite in the reserve, preferring to keep a distance from it. I will explain the reason for that later. I would never take my tourists anywhere near them. Before we approach them I want to tell you more about this particular tribe.'

He indicated a place to sit and we inspected it before sitting down. We removed our rucksacks and he handed out a few biscuits. We ate them silently and then he told me about the tribe we were about to meet, according to hearsay.

'All over South America there are tribes of indigenous Indians. Some live in the mountains, some on the plains and others here in the rain forests.' This first sentence was one he used to inform his normal parties of tourists and was uttered in a rote monotone. Now he addressed me as his friend.

'The Nucutanis of my childhood are a very small tribe, Martin. They are very friendly and were a target for the more aggressive larger tribes further north. There are great differences between all these tribes, both here and in the other countries of South America. It is much too complicated for me to try to explain. Perhaps when you return to England you can read about it. I will try to tell you in my simple way. Even now, there are still headhunters and cannibals amongst some. People are captured in raids and sacrificed in ceremonies. Languages and dialects are different from tribe to tribe. I understand the Nucutanis only because I was born here and have visited them many times. I left before my manhood initiation ceremony. The disfigurement that you will see on the young men here will shock you. Try not to give way to your normal feelings. Some of the older men have pierced noses and the women too have disfigurements. Some of these are to their private parts and I do not expect you to understand or agree. You must understand these tribes were isolated for centuries from the outside world. They were the world. Each tribe made laws and rules that gradually became more complicated by succeeding leaders who were all powerful. If they were evil leaders they would invent rituals for their own satisfaction. I have read at school about Hitler, Genghis Khan, Stalin and even religious leaders who have perverted people's minds to their own ends. It is no different amongst these isolated tribes. The leaders forced their will on the people.

Dancing and crude music is part of all native people all over the world. It is no different here. They do not work, as you know it. The men fish and hunt when they need food. The women make pots, weave baskets and cook. They are self-sufficient. Over the centuries they have discovered drugs and liquid potions equal to any you have tried or even read about. They enjoy the pleasures of these in their leisure time. They have also found medicines that cure all sorts of ailments and diseases. If someone recovered, it was a good medicine, if they died then they tried something else, Martin'. *It was no different, I thought, than Fleming, Lister or Madame Currie experimenting till they found cures for diseases, whether by accident or patience. José* continued.

'Polygamy is widely practiced. Here only the elders are allowed more than one wife.' He looked at me seriously. 'I will say no more, Martin. You will see things in the next few days that will upset you. I hope you will try to accept them with a smile. These people smile a lot. They enjoy their way of life. If you join in as your father did, you too will leave as he did, all in one piece and well-remembered.' He said this last remark with a smile, but I took it seriously. I respected him more each day as I travelled with him. He was a clever man. Good fortune had taken him from the forest and he had taken advantage of it. He was at ease with me and I've no doubt his party of tourists looked at him in awe. He was certainly more educated than I imagined at first sight. I must try to rid myself of this university snobbery. Before I came, Manaus was a mystery to me. It was a town in the middle of the Brazilian rainforest, peopled by heathens and uneducated foreigners. I reminded myself of some of its statistics. It is the capital of Amazonas state and has been since the 19th century. It's a very important port, reached by seagoing vessels from the Atlantic, and has been since that time. It has botanical and zoological gardens. There is a jungle park, as Philippe had pointed out. The National Research Institute of Amazonia is there. It houses a university and the Geographic and Historical Institute of Amazonas. The Adolpho Ducke is probably the world's largest botanical gardens. It has an international airport and the city contains half of the state's population; about a million and a half people. José was an example of the education system. Mine was improving.

José rose from the log and strapped on his backpack. He cupped his hands over his mouth and called out. It was reminiscent of Tarzan, who I'd seen on television in the old black and white films. It was all I could do to suppress a smile. As the sound echoed into the distance, an answering call came back; José's face broke into a satisfied beam. He was home. In no time at all, children were running towards us followed by their parents. Their obvious pleasure changed somewhat at the sight of me. They all stopped and stared. He had never brought tourists into their sanctuary before and they were taken aback. He muttered a few sentences in their language and pointed at me. They slowly surrounded me and one of the elders approached me. He was typical of most of the men in the circle. Small and skinny with a loose cloth wrapped around his private parts like the old-fashioned baby's nappy. His arms and legs were covered with scars and tattoos. He had a small bone through his nose and a ring through his top lip. Girls at home had rings in every part of their anatomy, so what's new? *Somehow I don't think they would stand the pain suffered by these insertions.*

He came closer and I was aware of his smell. This was different to my own stale sweat that I'd now become used to. These people kept clean in their own way. Realistically they couldn't wash regularly. There were no soaps or shampoos, as we have been persuaded to use by the manufacturers. This was an all-pervading jungle smell of decaying vegetation and fungi and it was inescapable. Centuries had made them inured to it. Strange to say, my own olfactory glands were already becoming accustomed to the jungle. José and I had not shaved of course, and both of us had a decent growth of beard. Such niceties were a chore we mutually chose to dispense with, and lessened the target area for the insects. It was noticeable that all members of this tribe were hairless, including the women. It was another distinction they had adapted and adhered to. It was something else that didn't need cleaning.

The elder touched my top lip and shouted something to José, laughing as he did so. I hoped he wasn't proposing I had it pierced at this early stage in our relationship. I picked out the word *Willy* several times from his dialogue. He and José spoke for several minutes and the latter interpreted for me.

'He was comparing you to your father and thought you would have a *bigode*, a moustache.' *I breathed a sigh of relief.* 'Everyone in the tribe called him Willy. This man's name is Tunaku and he welcomes you. I told him that your father had died and it was the reason for your visit.' After further touching and poking of my body, Tunaku backed away and another of the older men stepped forward to get a closer look at me.

'This is Ignata,' explained, José, 'and he wishes you to stay with him as your father did when he was here.' Ignata embraced me warmly and over his shoulder the rest of his people joined in the celebrations as if it were the homecoming of a long lost son. I was happy about that. It meant my father had been welcome among them and they had good memories of him. I too, it seemed, was welcome because of that. I had difficulty associating a sweating intrepid explorer mingling with these people with my memories of William Henry Lockwood, the stuffy barrister. Perhaps I never tried to understand him. I was too busy enjoying the pleasures that were forthcoming at his expense. The more I learned about him the more I admired him and the feeling of guilt overtook me once more.

With Tunaku leading we all went over to the longhouse. This was in the centre of the village and large enough to accommodate everyone. It was their communal kitchen and dining room for most of their activities. It became a social room in the evenings. They were one big family sharing everything there. Surrounding this building were small huts where each family slept. It reminded me of Victorian back-to-back terraces in England. Everyone knew everyone and doors were never locked. Now, safety chains and burglar alarms were the norm. There were no locks here of course; very few of the huts had doors!

I was led to one end of the longhouse that seemed to be the dining area. It was covered with mats. All the males of the tribe, including all the youths who were old enough to have gone through their initiation ceremony were here. I knew this, as all of them were sporting proof of the fact by facial piercings of one sort or another. Some of these would have been very painful to receive, that's for sure. To show their bravery, some had additional ones on other parts of the body that were in evidence. I expect loincloths hid even more painful ones. I tried not to think about it. We sat down.

Although we had only arrived a short time ago, everyone in the village was present; the jungle telegraph at its best. I felt like a film star or a visiting president. All eyes were on us. José and I were the honoured guests.

At the other end, the females began cooking and it wasn't long before the smell wafted down towards me. Like any other gathering in any other part of the world, drinks were passed around. I was handed a small earthenware pot containing a dark liquid. It smelled a bit like creosote but had a definite rum flavour. I sipped it cautiously, as José had warned me about its potency. My hosts had no such qualms. It was an excuse to get drunk and before long I saw its effect on them. Whatever it was, it would be a class 'A' drug in Britain. Their inhibitions evaporated and most of the older ones came over to me to get a closer look at the strange looking guest of honour. They jabbered away and poked me continually. José said they were telling me of their memories of *Willy* and how sad they were that he was dead. Even the younger ones had heard stories about him. Poking was a friendly gesture like shaking hands. I got the idea and quickly returned their prods. Soon I had many friends and even more bruises. I must tell my friends back home about this hands-on idea to break down stuffiness at cocktail parties. It would be a rewarding ceremony, especially with the girls.

By the expressions on all their faces, no one had a bad word for my father. Fortunately, José sat next to me and interpreted, although at times I felt I was getting the expurgated version from him. I detected rude gestures from some of the elders.

When I enquired of José what they meant he shrugged and dismissed it as if it was of no consequence. It was a male thing, he said.

'It's the sort of thing you would hear at your stag nights and rugby clubs.' I wasn't convinced and began to suspect William Lockwood of even more indiscretions when younger. Whatever would the rotary club think?

Finally the food arrived and although I had only consumed a couple of mouthfuls of their home brew I already felt at home, or pleasantly drunk as I would say the morning after a party. Most of the gathering ate off shallow baskets lined with skin or leaves. As guest of honour my food came on an earthenware dish. It was a vegetable stew with meat. A universal dish I suppose. The vegetables were all strange to me, and I had no idea what sort of meat it was and didn't ask José. He would have dismissed that too, I'm sure. The young girls served the food and, as most of them were topless, it certainly beat any university knees-up I'd been to. The children cleared the table in a non-stop stream during the festivities. Tunaku stood and made another speech of welcome, although I didn't understand a word – I'm sure he was slurring his words. But it was of no consequence. Then it was time for the dancing to begin.

First came the young girls and then the young men, separately of course. They were not allowed close contact with each other until they had passed their respective initiation ceremonies. My guide said that anyone caught transgressing this law was severely dealt with. That's one thing I suppose I was thankful for, otherwise I could have been severely dealt with several times whilst at Oxford.

By this time the wives joined their husbands and there was a general knees-up. I was fairly drunk after another couple of the local tipple and, after a demonstration, joined in the dancing.

It was a kind of line dance with everybody changing partners and becoming rather lewd at times, with very little left to the imagination. It was virtually an invitation for sex by one person to the other. I was touched in the lower region several times by females but didn't reciprocate. I wasn't taking any chances. I didn't want to upset their men folk. I knew they were one of the friendly tribes, but I'm sure there must be a taboo against strangers touching up their wives on the first night. And punishments, according to José, would not be twelve hours community service.

I noticed couples leaving the arena and the numbers dwindling. Even in the state I was in, my fuddled brain became aware that wife swapping was on the agenda. There was very little "goodnight, Harry and Rose". Couples got very amorous and sneaked off, waving to their normal partners. José said it was probably time for us to go to bed and he led me towards Ignata's hut. There was no one in and he shone his torch into one corner, indicating where we would sleep. It was where he always slept when he came here, he told me. Several animal skins were laid out for us to lie on. There was a roughly woven cloth sheet for each of us. I took off my boots, lay down, pulled one of the sheets over me and was asleep in no time.

Chapter 10

I stirred and looked at my watch. It was ten o'clock and a thin shaft of light filtered through the opening of the hut. I was alone. I heard the familiar noises that I was now becoming used to. It seemed I had been left to sleep off my drunken stupor; José and the villagers would know the effect of their brew on a stranger. It was the worst hangover I had ever experienced. More than that, I felt sick, and the twisting in my stomach told me that my bowels were about to explode. Without stopping to put on my boots, I ran outside and made for the forest at the edge of the clearing. I squatted down over the nearest fallen log, there was always one available as a toilet. I didn't even have time to inspect what danger lay beneath my backside. I erupted from both ends at the same time. My head swam and the vomiting continued long after my stomach was empty. The diarrhoea eventually subsided. I sat there for some time in case it returned and then became aware of the presence of various insects at my rear end. I snatched up a leaf and wiped them away. I staggered back towards the collection of huts and passed out. Through the haze as I went down I saw José and Ignata. To my shame, they had probably witnessed it all.

When I awoke, they were both standing over me. I was back under the rough blanket but naked. I knew immediately that I had been washed all over and a cool cloth lay across my forehead. Ignata's wife Tamulin came over and held out her hand. In it were a handful of seeds and José told me to sit up and swallow them. He gave me a pot of liquid to help them down. It tasted vile but calmed my stomach in an instant. The seeds must have been a powerful sedative for I fell asleep once more.

The next time I woke up it was if it had all been a dream. I felt marvellous and ravenously hungry. This time it was the figure of Havuana, Ignata's granddaughter who was kneeling over me. The first thing I noticed was the circle tattooed on her forehead. Quite a few of the young women had similar ones and I had meant to ask José the reason for them. She was bare breasted and quite beautiful but at the moment food was uppermost in my mind. Even so, under the rough sheet, my body responded to what my eyes saw. It was as if my initial thoughts on waking had been read, because she held a plate of fruits and what looked like a chicken leg but much larger. It didn't taste like turkey or duck so I imagined it was most likely a parrot of some sort. I sat up and stripped it down to the bone, sampling the fruit in between. Before she went and before I had chance to thank her, she passed a jug of liquid over and off she went. It was cold and tasted a little of pineapples. My clothes had been washed and dried and lay beside me. I dressed slowly, not believing I could have recovered so quickly. José told me later that I'd been out for twenty-four hours. No wonder I was hungry.

Ignata, his family and José were outside as if waiting for me. I looked sheepishly at them expecting at least a little chiding for what they had witnessed. Back home I would never had heard the last of it. There was none. It was if the whole episode was forgotten. I sensed the whole tribe had been waiting for my appearance for they were gathered in the background. As I appeared, the waiting crowd cheered.

'Are you ready for that special outing I promised you yesterday?' said José. I vaguely remembered him saying it was initiation day for some of the young men and that I could join them. I felt honoured and agreed. I felt fit enough for anything and at the back of my mind was a feeling of satisfaction. I had almost completed my mission. I had returned to where my father had been all those years ago. I had seen the sights of the forest as he had, and if I'd read the signs right, José was pleased with my performance alongside him. I had met the people of those faded photographs from a time when my father was roughly my age. I had been feted by them and been guest at a party in my own honour. I'd got drunk and had the worst hangover in my life. I'd got over it and now here I was about to join them for the day in a very special ceremony. I had never felt so elated. I was certainly in no rush to return home. I nodded and said, 'Let's get to it, José.'

With the initiates leading and their fathers following we all trooped into the forest, José and I at the rear. The path petered out and then the young men hacked away at the undergrowth. This first part, said José, was to prove that they could use their machetes proficiently. It was counter-productive to tracking down a quarry. The noise they made would scare off quarry. This would come later. I had already seen the various weapons of the Nucutani tribe. They had blowpipes, bows and arrows and small spears. The spears were really for defence in case of a charge by a wild boar or a male deer. The main weapon used by the Nucutanis for the hunting is the bow and arrow. It's ideal for bringing down small monkeys and birds from the canopy and most of the men become skilled in its use. The arrows were tipped with poison just as I'd read about at school.

For the initiation outing the spear is felt to be more arduous and shows extra bravery. The youths participating had a machete in their left hands for clearing the undergrowth and a small spear in the right. Their task was to track down a small pig or red deer and kill it. They carried their bows around their shoulders. The ritual had now become symbolic over the centuries. One of them would be lucky enough to bring down such an animal, then all of them would have a hand in its final demise and death. This meant they all qualified for manhood. That way only one unfortunate beast met its demise. As José said, they didn't kill for the sake of killing. At the end of the initiation day all the tribe would benefit. It was a tradition and had been refined over the years to meet all the criteria necessary.

I stuck close to José and a torturous couple of hours passed with no one talking. When they reached a clearing, the young men would stop using the machetes. Then it was time to carefully make their way through the undergrowth quietly so as not to alarm their quarry. Eventually one of the youths was victorious and we heard his shout of triumph. He emerged from the darkness of the trees with his prize. Then he and the rest of the young men set about cutting up the carcase. It was a small deer and more kudos was attached to it than a pig; this was evident from the screams of delight from the youths and the applause from the elders.

José and I trailed behind them as they each carried their trophy back to the village as proof. Their young bodies were now blood-smeared, some of it deliberate as they had laughed during the slaughter. As they entered the village they were met with wild cheers by the rest of the tribe.

The youth who had been the one to kill the animal took the head as his trophy. It was he who led the procession and was crowned king of the initiates for a day as a reward. In the evening came the tattoo ceremony. A male relative, usually the father, scratched a phallic symbol into the side of his charge's neck and rubbed in a red dye. They displayed this proudly afterwards to any girl that took their fancy. The winner with the head, of course, got first choice for his bride. This again was a symbolic gesture that some chief in the past had thought was a good idea. Now it was just part of the ritual. He would have already chosen someone that had taken his fancy beforehand. Choices are usually decided before their trial in the forest. There are no jealousies. They accept the decisions of their elders at an early age.

The girls also go through their own ritual before they qualify as women and become qualified to mother children.

This is an even longer process starting when they are quite young and takes several years. Finally, she comes before the *Laikia*, an older woman who is chosen each year by the others. She examines the girl to see if she is pure and will make a good wife. Then a circle is tattooed on her forehead. I now understood the reason for the circle I had seen on the head of Havuana. José told me all this as we returned to the village.

'Sounds good to me,' I replied, tongue in cheek, 'you know what you're getting. It could be a good subject for the Oxford debating society.'

I felt pleased to be privy to their customs. Very few tourists would be. Because of my father and José, I had been accepted into the tribe without question. I felt somehow I had become a member of these people. On this particular day the young men who had taken part in killing the deer were getting more and more excited as they approached the village. No wonder, I thought. They were probably thinking of their reward at the end of the night and imagining the girl of their dreams sharing a bed with them. Maybe it was my vivid imagination. When we reached the village, I had to tell José all that was on my mind about my stay here and how much I owed to him.

'I have now seen most of the wildlife in the rainforest, and have enjoyed meeting your relatives and friends. I have been amazed at their local customs and knowledge of natural medicines; today's ceremony has topped it all. I have accomplished much more than I thought I would when I set out from England. I am now ready to return to Manaus and then home. The only animal I haven't seen is the jaguar and sightings are very rare, so I am not too disappointed.' He was pleased with what I said but I think my mention of the jaguar remained a sore point with him.

'Of course my good friend, you have done well and your father would be proud of you. Tonight's celebrations will be something more to tell your friends at home. I am sure you will enjoy the ceremony of the young boys as they become men.'

Chapter 11

Parents and elders joined in the wild cries of the hunting party as we returned to the village. The young men carried their trophies into the long hut and laid them down ready for the women to prepare them for the evening celebrations. Their job done, they went back to their own families to brag about their part in the hunt. Then everyone would prepare for the evening. José and I returned to our lodgings and talked about it. Later we got ready for the evening performance, and I was excited once more at what new events I would be privileged to witness.

The atmosphere went strangely quiet as José and I made our entrance into the long hut. I thought the focus would be on the young men and that my feting would be over. As it was, I sensed that all eyes were on us and there were murmurings from the elders who stood separately, as befitted their rank. I had the distinct feeling I was the topic of conversation. It appeared that I was still the honoured guest as far as they were concerned. Initiation ceremonies happened regularly; my arrival was something special, or so it seemed. After we were seated properly and after a moment or so, the elders raised their hands in unison and the celebrations got under way.

The young men went through their ordeal one by one as I had been told they would previously, culminating in the tattoo on the side of their necks. It was a small price to pay for what they would receive in return from the girl of their choice. The piercing of the lips would be done at a later date. There were the usual lewd gestures that I had come to recognise from the older men. By now there was no need for an interpreter to understand what it all meant. The sheepish grins from the young men only confirmed what they all expected.

The women entered with the food as before and more ribald remarks came from them. The musicians came in with their bamboo pipes and drums made from the skins of various animals. These had been stretched over wooden frames; the hooves had been fashioned into elaborate drumsticks. There was no end to the ingenuity of these people.

Then the festivities commenced. Young girls came round with gourds of various brews and the ones with the circles on their foreheads seem to get more than their share of attention from the newly initiated young men. As the night wore on some of them disappeared as couples. Havuana and another girl came and sat next to José and me. I had seen her in his company several times since we'd arrived. She too had the circle on her forehead and I was surprised she was not coupled with some young initiate. She was beautiful and I thought she would have been snapped up. When I mentioned this to Jose, he simply said he was her uncle and she always looked forward to his visits and fussed around him.

He warned me what drinks to avoid if I didn't want a repeat of what had happened last time and I really began to enjoy the festivities. The music finally stopped, the fires died down and the villagers left in their family groups. As they left, each one came over and made gestures or smiled. It was very touching and I felt slightly drunk, but no more than a few pints at the Dog and Duck. I even said I was sorry to be leaving. I suppose it sounded maudlin due to the booze and I hoped it didn't appear patronising when José interpreted it to them. They seemed to appreciate it by their joyful expressions. It reminded me of my last night at Oxford. Eventually José called a halt to our evening.

'I think we should go too, Martin,' he said. The two girls rose and followed us, Havuana staying close to me. Outside, there was a full moon. The air was clear and more temperate than I had experienced since leaving home. It seemed fitting for my last night with these people that the weather should be kind. The atmosphere was almost like the last night of a holiday in Spain. As for my hosts, I had enjoyed their hospitality and they had taken me in as if I belonged there. José who had made it all possible turned to me.

'I shall not be sleeping with you tonight, my friend,' he said, and I detected a satisfied smile even in the moonlight. He and his "niece" disappeared into one of the huts. I saw now why he was in a hurry to leave the party. Havuana took hold of my hand and steered me towards another. My heart pounded. I had not expected this, even though Havuana's beauty had not escaped my notice. I was simply surprised that she too, had no partner for the night. It was pitch black inside but a shaft of moonlight revealed coconut mats strewn across the floor. They were freshly prepared and smelled good. She motioned for me to go in first; it was the custom. The man had to see if it was safe. As she entered she dropped her wrap-around skirt and

148

her naked body was silhouetted in the opening. It matched the top half I hadn't failed to notice before. I heard her movements as she moved around the hut in the darkness and then lights appeared from three pots of oil as she lit the wicks. Pleasant perfumes filled the air. One of them I'm sure was to repel mosquitoes, as I was never disturbed by any throughout our night of lovemaking. Perhaps some of the drinks were spiked with aphrodisiacs but I was insatiable, waking several times during the night to repeat the experience. She was eager each time and ready to find different ways to excite me. I was always ready to reciprocate.

I was alone when I awoke the next morning. Maybe it had been a dream from some hallucinogenic drink I had downed the night before. There was no Havuana and no candles, but if I closed my eyes I could still smell her and hear her moans. The sex had certainly been real too.

I made my way to the hut where I had slept on that first night. The big Brazilian was alone and waiting for me, already packed. He handed me my own backpack. He made no mention of the previous night. There was no innuendo, no knowing winks. It had all been arranged without my knowledge no doubt, but it had been pure and romantic. It was certainly not like one of my one-night stands.

'We'll go over to the longhouse, get some breakfast and then we will be off,' he said, his face impassive. We ate the food in silence. I looked across at him but I could have been just another tourist. We headed towards the path that lead out of the village and back to his boat. One or two of the villagers waved happily as they went about their business. There was no sign of Ignata or Tunaku and I was disappointed. After what

I had experienced on arrival and the non-stop parties and ceremonies, I expected the whole village to turn out for my departure. Perhaps I'd misread it. Perhaps we'd called at festival time and I was lucky. The party was over for them and they were all going about their normal routine.

The return journey was a bit of an anti-climax for the first few hours as there was very little new for José to make a comment on. Little had changed in the various paths during those few days. The task took less out of us than it had done on the outward journey but equally there was less reward to look forward to as before. When we stopped for rests I attempted to break down his silence but it was an effort. He looked thoughtful and I sensed there was something on his mind. Perhaps he knew about my night with Havuana and was angry. Perhaps he thought I had taken advantage of the generosity of his people. I waited till after our first proper stop for food and we had eaten.

'Is there something on your mind, José?' I said, defensively. His brow furrowed but he remained silent and shook his head with a half-hearted no; I persisted.

'Is it to do with Havuana?' I said more firmly, a little affronted by this new attitude towards me. He drew in a deep breath.

'I can see I shall have to tell you the truth, Martin. What you experienced last night was planned as soon as you arrived and the villagers knew who you were. Most of what you experienced was for your benefit and it led up to last night with you and Havuana getting together. I was part of their plot and perhaps I feel guilty, however much you may have enjoyed it.'

He waited for this to sink in before he continued. Although it was midday, he reached for a bottle of some potent drink supplied by our hosts. He withdrew the stopper and drank heavily, then passed it to me, indicating for me to do the same.

'Drink first, Martin, for I have more things to tell you.'

It was almost an order. I silently did as I was told. As the liquid did its job I had time to think of what other revelations he had for me. I had obviously been kept in the dark by one and all during my visit here. I needed the truth. He waited for the spirit to take effect before he continued. It wasn't long before I started to feel the full effects. It was if he was a doctor and about to give me the results of his diagnosis and I was slightly sedated.

'The Nucutanis,' he began, 'like a lot of the rainforest tribes, live in isolation. Centuries ago, they would attack each other and carry off young girls to bring new blood into their own village. This was to stop inbreeding. Despite their primitive way of life, they had learned about the results of incest. This practice still exists but the Nucutanis are a small tribe and always came off worst. That is why they moved away from being exploited by the more warlike tribes. Unfortunately because of this, in succeeding generations the children were becoming weaker because of it. The elders decided it would be better if chosen strangers were invited to father children with the fittest young girls.' He saw the change in my expression as I quickly jumped to conclusions.

'Before you say anything, let me finish, Martin. This was happening before I was born. Any lucky explorer or tourist that happened to wander near to the village enjoyed hospitality they never expected. They were blindfolded and kidnapped. After spending an uncomfortable night as prisoner they were in terror of their lives, some of them no doubt thinking their days were numbered. They were very much surprised to be offered the alternative of a young maiden for the night or having their throats cut. Of course the elders vetted them before they had the pleasure of a night of sex. It was a hit and miss affair until I grew up in Manaus and started my trips into the rainforest. I was asked to single out tourists that would make the best fathers.' He saw the resentment building up in my eyes. 'You were different of course, because of everyone's fondness for *Willy.*' I finally managed to speak. By this time the drink had taken its effect and I remembered my all-night session with the lovely Havuana. I'd had a lot of pleasure and it hadn't cost me one Real. No one twisted my arm.

'Fair enough, José, but you're assuming Havuana becomes pregnant. And that would only be one new addition to your people. Not much of a dividend for all other benefits I received while I stayed there.' I tried to sound blasé about the whole deception. I pointed out the outlay and the poor dividends, if any.

'Not quite, Senhor Lockwood junior,' he said smiling, 'you made love several times during the night, *sim*? Each time you woke it was a new fertile young woman, specially chosen by the *Laikia* and most likely to become a *mãe*. In the darkness and covered in the same perfumed oils you could not tell one from another *sim*? And of course they didn't speak so how could you know it was a different girl. Don't tell me you were disappointed?' It was a rhetorical question and he laughed. In a way I felt honoured. How many offsprings had I sired? How many young Martins would there be walking through the forest in twenty years' time? A thought struck me.

'And was my father one of those chosen by the elders all those years ago?' I asked.

By this time I was beginning to see the funny side of it. I had visions of the girls waiting till I dozed off and changing places. The next one would wake me and so on. It seemed incongruous that William Henry Lockwood, would-be barrister had been in the same situation. I came back to reality and looked up, José's face was serious.

'*Willy,* as he is fondly remembered by the villagers was my *Pai*.' He knew my Portuguese was good enough to understand that. He waited as everything fell into place in my mind. The hairs on the back of my neck stood out. Ever since I first saw him there had been something about his looks that had nagged at my brain. And of course his lighter skin. I had always guessed he had European ancestry. But so many countries had invaded or emigrated here that it was not extraordinary. Now I knew why. I was trying to figure out all these revelations when he broke into my thoughts.

'It was different with your father. Unlike the others before him he had made the expedition with local bearers. They had been part of the Nucutani tribe and worked in the dock area in Manaus. He engaged them as porters for his one-man expedition and they could tell he was a genuine explorer. He asked them many questions about the rainforest people and he was genuinely interested in their plight. It was easy for them to lead him to the village. He wasn't kidnapped. He must have been surprised at first to find how welcome he was. He stayed for some time and learned their ways. He fell in love with my mother when she had just become a woman and I was their only child. He returned to England to settle his affairs intending to return and take us both back with him. Sadly she died shortly after he left. He arrived back too late to say goodbye to her and he was heartbroken. He couldn't settle here without her. My uncle Magnuka – that is my mother's brother – had gone to work in Manaus with his wife and two small boys. My father tracked him down. He persuaded him to take me into his own family and to bring me up with his own children. He then returned to England and sent money every month for my upbringing and education. It was only a small amount at the beginning but it helped my uncle too. He has always been grateful for it. As your father became richer he increased the money. That is why we all had a good education. Your father, *our father*, was a good man, Martin. I would have known nothing about any of this; I was too young to remember him when he left. I always thought I was my uncle's child. But one day I was having an argument with a brother and he told me the truth to upset me. I asked my uncle if it was true and he told me the whole story.

When I grew up I wanted to go and visit him. My uncle told me he had married again and had a son with a new wife. He said, "Their lives are completely different to ours and you will be out of place. Your appearance will upset your father and his new family. It is better you remain here with us." I have tried to forget him. Then *Senhora Sorte* led you to Philippe Sousa and then to my uncle.' *Lady luck indeed*, I thought. *It was to my benefit too.*

Suddenly I realised what José had known all along. We were half-brothers. For him, our journey to the Nucutanis from Manaus had not been about an exploration into the rainforest and its inhabitants. He had wanted to show me the place where our father had found his first love. All the time he must have been observing me, seeing what kind of person was his half-brother, and I was unaware of this. During the journey he must have approved of me, and which was why we developed that affinity.

There was now a different relationship between the two of us as far as I was concerned. No longer did I treat him as a friendly guide I had engaged for my mission. I was now eager to help with all the chores as two brothers would. I could see he was pleased to see how I had reacted to his revelations.

He sensed my new attitude towards him, gave me more responsibility and continued to teach me all he had learned. At mealtimes we laughed and joked in the same vein. The return journey was no longer a contract.

With renewed energy from this new relationship, and our new bond we hacked our way back to the boat. In no time at all it seemed we were in clear water and on the last leg of the journey to Manaus.

Soon we were floating gently with the current in the wide river, away from the deafening sound of the hostile clamour that still reached us with the volume turned down. I had time to assess this new relationship. It was my turn to see him in a new light. At the beginning of the journey he knew all about me. Before, I was merely admiring his skills. It was my turn to see him in a different light. I suddenly had a brother, albeit a half-brother. No longer was I an only child.

We were a day out from Manaus and the opportunity to tell him what was on my mind presented itself. It was something that had grown like a seed in my brain and now wanted to bloom in the open air. As usual he was smoking his last cigar of the evening and we were mellowed from our usual nightcap. The sounds from the forest had quietened just a little and I was waiting for an opening. I mentioned some of the sights, including the flora and fauna, that had made the journey memorable for me that his skill had made possible. I stared across till I caught his eye.

'It's a pity a Jaguar never showed itself,' I said with a sly smile as if to chide him. 'It would have been a perfect trip.' We could talk this way now; we were equals. I don't mean equal in rank or class, I'm not a snob in that sense. I'd never felt superior to him. No, it wasn't that. We were of the same family; I think we could now argue without resentment. He responded in the same manner.

'Perhaps we could go again and we will have better luck next time, Martin. I have always wanted to go further into the rain forests. There are unexplored places I have heard about from the old men in the village when I have been among them. At least half a dozen of our father's photos are not taken in the village of the Nucutanis. I am sure they were taken much further into the reservation. I have never been able to venture there with my tourists.' He emphasised the word 'tourist' as if I was not one of them.

He said "*our father*" quite naturally. But of course he'd always been our father to José from the moment we had first met. It was I who had to get used to the fact. He continued. 'He must have journeyed much further north into the reserve before or after he came upon the Nucutani village. The men in those photos have different tribal markings to the

156

Nucutanis. I think they are a war-like people. Tunaku has told me terrible stories about them when I have visited. He said it was the reason he and all the others had moved to the very edge of the reserve, away from them. Of course I dismissed these stories as threats to keep the children from wandering too far into the forest on their own. You too must have stories of bogeymen for the same reason.' I nodded.

'True,' I said, but I pointed out the scar I'd seen on my father's arm in those pictures. 'I thought it had been done like a tattoo when my father was perhaps drunk one night.' He shook his head.

'It is unlike anything the Nucutanis do,' he replied seriously.

'This means that his journey was after his stay with your people. He has no scar in those photographs has he?' I said convincingly. He agreed with a nod.

'True, there was something else Magnuka told me and his own children as we grew up that could now make sense.' I listened as he explained.

'As we grew older and could understand about such things he told us that parties of men from this tribe would snatch young baby boys in the night from small tribes. They would be brought up as their own without knowing otherwise. In this way they would have healthy stock. It was something that all small tribes were worried about. It is of course, what the Nucutani elders did, only in a much friendlier way, eh, Martin?' he added with a grin. We seemed to be solving all the mysteries in the photos and getting to learn more about William Lockwood's journey years ago.

'Now that we understand all these things, perhaps you and I should try to go there and satisfy ourselves it was the place where our father went. I certainly want to, how about you, Martin? It would certainly beat my usual trips for the tourists. We could share the cost,' he concluded, as if to remove any doubts that may have crept in about the reason for going. I knew him well enough now to know he had no ulterior motive for another expedition. It was what I'd been waiting for and perhaps in hindsight, he too.

'I am definitely game for it now, José,' I said without preamble. 'I think I've conquered my everyday fears of the nasties in the forests. This sounds exciting and dangerous too.' His excitement became obvious too.

'Then what are we waiting for Martin, my brother?' We talked of little else till we reached Manaus.

He tied up his beloved boat and ensured it was as secure as possible at his landing space. There was an unspoken agreement among the tourist operators to keep an eye on the boats and equipment of the rest. Petty thieves were unlikely on that section of the river; they usually kept to the town and picked on tourists. There would be short thrift for any of them if they were caught stealing from hire boats. The police too, would be equally severe with them. Jose's battered car was waiting under the coolness of the trees not far away. Despite wanting to seek the luxury of a hotel on my return it would have been churlish to turn down his offer of accommodation while we prepared for our forthcoming return to the rainforest. We had lived together for almost two weeks in the worst conditions possible. I had no qualms about that. And he was my brother. I realised we could eat together and sleep together without any awkwardness in the future. So, as it drew dark we arrived at his small flat on the outskirts of Manaus.

Chapter 12

The hotel where I had stayed on my arrival in Manaus had a warning that it could be unsafe to venture out at night alone. I had read about the Favelos but took some of it with a pinch of salt. I thought it might be to keep the tourists spending money in the hotel bar. I glimpsed some of these tin shacks and their inhabitants on the way to José's accommodation and I could see the need for such a warning. My half-brother's flat was some distance away in this booming city; it was part of a complex for the wage-earning workers from the many factories much in evidence. The flats were fairly modern and purpose built with shops at ground level and parking facilities. A few hundred yards away there was a school and a park containing a children's playground. It was well-planned for the economically thriving Brazil. Manaus was reaping the benefits despite the pollution it was creating. For the time being, the politicians were sweeping the Favelos and its problems under the carpet: Brazil's economy was all-important.

The flat was small, reminding me very much of urban flats for the local population in Spain and Portugal. When on holiday in those places I always wondered why it was necessary to box people up when the countries have much more room than we have in Britain. Gardens are practically unheard of.

Despite being away from it for long periods of time, José's flat was clean and tidy. It was only what I expected from him. The only smell was redolent of his favourite cigar by which I was now used to. It was late September, but the heat was almost as humid as in the rainforest when we arrived back in Manaus. The block of flats was stifling from the day's heat and José opened the windows. They would have been shut for security reasons while he was away. He would be used to the atmosphere so opening them was more likely for my benefit.

'In the winter months we often get a cool wind from the south at night. It is called a *friagem* and is very welcome.' I wasn't so lucky. He opened the small fridge-freezer and, true to his efficiency, there were frozen baguettes and cheese. He took out two bottles of ice-cold Mexican lager and took the tops off. He handed me one and we each took a long swig.

'That will do for now. I think we will eat first, Martin; our sweat can wait till after. It will be all the more satisfying when we get rid of it.' He put two more lagers on the table unopened and in a few minutes we were wolfing down the food. I could never have envisaged when I left England that at the end of a journey on the other side of the world I would be so happy, despite smelling like the inside of a rugby player's jock strap. It had been a satisfying trip in more ways than one, and through it I had practically experienced a growing up that couldn't be learned at a university.

We ate in silence, beaming at each other; it was heaven. Sitting in comfort with no insects, eating fresh cheese baguettes and sipping an ice-cold drink. The elation continued later as José showed me the bathroom. There was no bath, just a shower. He took his clothes off and threw them into a small cupboard in the kitchen. He motioned to me to do the same. I followed him under the shower that he'd already turned on and adjusted and we stood there as the clean warm water cascaded down on the pair of us. We had no inhibitions. We'd spent too much time in each other's company in awful conditions not to worry about being together in a shower. We were also brothers. He was the first to exit and once more I followed. He produced two large towels embroidered with Pelé that had seen better days; Pelé's smile had faded somewhat. He had been loath to part with them for obvious reasons. They were scrupulously clean and still with enough fluff to do a good job. We dried ourselves off. He produced two dressing gowns, one was an old one that he treasured and felt comfortable in. The second was a birthday present intended to replace it. It was for me. He turned on the radio and found a local non-stop music station. The music was Brazilian and interspersed with commercials for local businesses. We never spoke about our proposed exploration. It was completely forgotten in our euphoria. Later on I was treated to more of his hospitality and we got drunk before finally turning in. It was a double bed despite the small bedroom and his bachelor status. He read my thoughts.

'I sometimes get lucky,' he said by way of explanation before he switched the light off. Sleep followed immediately. There would be no fresh bites to remind me of nocturnal visitors in the morning.

Chapter 13

I suppose the satisfaction of my accomplished journey into the rainforest, and the discovery that my guide was related meant I had an untroubled mind. I slept soundly. The cheese made me dream but most of them were pleasant. A thousand images whirled around. Havuana featured prominently in some of them. The other partners of that night all had her face.

It was nine o'clock when I felt the need to relieve my bladder and I was the only occupant of the bed. I smelled strong Brazilian coffee and bacon and it was heaven. José had been to the shops situated beneath us and the breakfast was an improvement on the continental one I would have had at a hotel. He said very little and we ate breakfast. As if by habit, we cleared away together and then sat down obviously of the same mind; to discuss our future trip. Despite our light-hearted manner on the previous day we had both been serious about it. It was I who spoke first.

'You know this proposed trip is no longer about sighting a jaguar José?' I said. 'I was only joking.'

'I know, Martin. We have changed in such a short time, you and I. Of course I knew you were my brother and had the advantage. I did feel a little more responsible for your safety of course, than usual. From the beginning you were friendlier towards me than my usual tourists. I was so pleased with that. You put more effort into the trip than any of them. From the start you never acted superior like most of my other paying customers. We became friends because of that. Finally you learned you were my brother and you were happy about that. We were destined to meet. Even so I will still educate you in the ways of survival and treat you to even more sights that they do not have on this Eden Project that you talk about.' It was a short speech, delivered fluently as if rehearsed. He had thought deeply about it. He laughed and continued seriously.

'From the beginning you wanted to learn about the forest. You wanted to do things to help me. I enjoyed teaching you, and you learned quickly.' I stopped him before I became embarrassed.

'I've thought about little else since we came back and this is what I propose, José.'

He looked slightly taken aback for a second so I quickly explained. 'First of all, it is your boat so I will pay for all the fuel. We will probably have to take extra fuel because of the distance. I will leave you to work all that out. We will take enough bread to last us till we reach the places we visited on our last journey, or some other town on the way. There we will replenish our fresh items. We're not tied down by time and are free to do or go as we please. Again I'll leave all that planning to you. We can do the same on the return journey if we survive.' I laughed.

'During our last journey I could see that the forest provided us with most of the other foods and that was no problem. Wild vegetables seem to be your speciality and there were no shortages. Fish seem to be waiting to be caught even by me, and I enjoyed catching them. The only thing missing from our diet was meat and, as we will be travelling more on foot through the forest we could include it on our menu. It would be nice if I could taste something from the wide variety I saw before. I'm sure there are small animals that will not deplete the stocks,' I added, remembering his remarks about not taking more out of the forest than was needed. He nodded and smiled.

'And how do you propose catching them, Martin?' he asked, beaming.

'Easy,' I replied. 'When we go into Manaus to get our supplies, I intend to buy a rifle with your help. It only needs to be a 2.2, I hope that won't be a problem?' I said questioningly. 'I fancied going to Sandhurst and become an officer in the army while at Oxford. It was a passing whim; I hate discipline. I even took a course on the rifle range. Did quite well actually. With your tracking skills and culinary prowess, we can have some tasty meals.' I stopped talking and waited for a reply. 'Now it's your turn. What are your priorities, José, and do you agree with all I've said? If not, what have you come up with?'

He had listened carefully and his gentle nodding throughout seemed to indicate there were no objections. He could see that I had thought carefully about it.

'Perhaps the gun may be the only problem, Martin. We will go to a second-hand shop in the poorer quarter that seems to sell everything, legal or otherwise. It would be nice to eat meat for a change on such a long journey. As far as I can see we will need very few food supplies on the trip. Most of it is there for the asking. It will not be like my usual trips. I shall get a larger supply of tinned goods including biscuits, just in case. All these dry goods are obtainable in tins. For obvious reasons everything has to be in tins, of course. Where we are going the wildlife can smell a crumb if it is exposed to the air. I'll take extra medicines, and as food supplies are light because there are only two of us, and a paraffin stove might come in handy in an emergency. It is useful for a light at night and helps to keep away unwanted guests.' He was referring to creatures and not people. 'It will be a long journey so we must be ready for everything.' As the morning passed we added little items to the list as they came to mind. We both felt a sense of excitement by lunchtime.

José had worn his normal clothes from his wardrobe that morning when he got dressed. I'd kept the old robe on, as his clothes were too big for me, not that it mattered. He'd washed and dried our jungle-weary clothes and was about to iron them. I stopped him.

'I intend to start this exploration with new gear,' I said, 'and that goes for you too. It's the least I can do.' I shrugged away his protests. I went on to explain that I wasn't short of money and left it at that. Because I'd been to university and never worked, he'd assumed I was rich. I had grown to trust him and he was my half-brother, but I didn't see the need to tell him of my inheritance, the amount would have overwhelmed him. By rights I suppose being the first-born he was entitled to the lot, or at least half of it. But as my father had sent money for his education and not left him anything in his will, perhaps he thought he'd done sufficient. I had been the son he'd been closest to despite our apparent coolness towards each other.

He had never married his first love and probably put it down to a youthful fling later in his life, as he became a barrister. It was best to leave it at that. Perhaps my father had misgivings about what the Rotary Club would have thought about his youthful philandering with native girls in the rainforests of Brazil, had his will named José. My thoughts returned to the matter in hand and the man opposite. I dismissed any more conjectures.

'I'll get dressed in my old clothes now that they are clean and we'll go into town and get new ones for us both. I'll change in the outfitters and dump my old ones. Then when I'm looking decent we'll get something to eat at a nice restaurant with air-conditioning. We'll have a slap-up meal with wine and I'll spare no expense. Maybe we can remember it when we are eating the insides of some small mammal surrounded by insects after their share. Then this afternoon we'll see about getting equipped for everything we need for our return to the wild.' He could see my mind was made up and had no argument.

With outstretched hand and a typical Latin shrug of the shoulders, he smiled. He didn't need to speak. We were a happy pair looking forward to our next adventure. I only hope the outcome warranted the preparation and would be as satisfying as the last.

There was no rush to return. The rainforest has been there for a long time and wasn't going away. We took a couple of days carefully completing our list of essentials and I could see that José was enjoying not having to seek bargains. I was with him on all his shopping expeditions and insisted on the best quality of whatever we needed.

Manaus is a huge city and has slowly spread outwards since its early beginnings, during the rubber boom a century before. José showed me more of it than on my first visit. We paid a brief visit to the science museum that is housed in a huge grove. Here was the place that Philippe Sousa had told me about. In it was a large selection of forest flora and fauna that I'd seen in the wild. They were much less intimidating. We didn't stay long. It would take a week to enjoy all that they had to offer in the INPA, which is the acronym for the science museum – full name: Instituta de Pesquisas da Amazonia. It also houses a herbarium, one of the largest collections of plants in Brazil, with over a hundred thousand species. José was quick to point out other buildings that are available to the residents of Manaus; most of them dating back to those century-old prosperous days. The Rio Negro Palace Cultural Centre was the Government Headquarters from as far back as 1918. The Teatro Amazonas had the appearance of a Greek temple from the outside with a huge dome on the top. Apart from the timber from the local forest, most of the materials were shipped from Europe. The iron columns supporting the roof were from Scotland and are painted to look like marble. I listened enthralled as José excitedly told me about all the magnificent buildings in this great city. He could see I was interested in the history of it. I could have looked it up in an Encyclopaedia before I came but being shown them by my own personal guide was the real thing. It was a marvellous two days for both of us after our trip into the rainforest. I enjoyed his tour guide of the city, and he enjoyed the food and wines of restaurants to which I insisted on taking him. Ones he rarely visited normally. At the end of the two days we were refreshed and both satisfied with the equipment for our proposed journey into the unknown. We spent the last night at his flat having a quiet night in listening to music and went to bed early.

Chapter 14

Despite it only being a few weeks since we began that first journey, I noticed subtle changes in the terrain, even through the places we had travelled before. The rainforests are subject to dramatic changes due to the heavy storms and erosion caused by the torrent of water continuously tearing at the banks on the bends in the river. Trees are swept away and new greenery springs up where silt has built up on the opposing bank. It still amazes me, this force of nature that has persisted for thousands of years. I'm continually in wonder of how the land, the people and the creatures in and around the waters adapt to the ever-changing terrain. I'm overawed by the power of the rivers as they make their way to the sea, as they inevitably do, and have done for millions of years. I have been on rivers in Europe and they seem to meander along carrying the occasional twig or leaf in their wake. How different the Rio Negro and the Amazon, carving through the land, forever changing its shape. José had mapped out our route on a sheet before we came and discussed it with me. It was sheathed in a plastic sleeve; otherwise the humid atmosphere would have made it unreadable in no time. He didn't need my input and he wasn't patronising me. It was he said, in case anything happened to him; at least I would have some idea where I was.

'You have learned enough about the sun and stars on that first journey. You know how to use a compass, that much I have seen. You know a little of the medicines, and you are an excellent fisherman,' he laughed. 'You recognise the fruits that we eat and you are now aware of the many dangers. You probably know more than I do about the motor. You are a quick learner, Martin. I think there is little danger of you getting lost.' I had no response to such praise.

Our first stop was by virtue of the same stretch of the Rio Negro and we were staying overnight as we did before at Aiparuca. We saw the smoke haze of the town in the distance.

I was so relaxed on the first few nights I couldn't believe it. I compared the two experiences, then and now. Then, the noise from the wildlife unnerved me and I was apprehensive of spending a night surrounded by them. My guide was a stranger and I could have had my throat cut as I slept. A little dramatic perhaps, but I wasn't a happy young man. I feared I had made a terrible mistake leaving Cornwall and a life of luxury, now that I had my inheritance. This time I was almost blasé about the overnight stay. We reached the outskirts of Aiparuca and José looked for a suitable camping area. The day had been uneventful with the exception of a few new bird species. One of them was very unusual and called a hoatzin. It was known as the laughing falcon and looked almost prehistoric, with blue facial skin and red eyes. There was a flock of them and they squawked noisily from the bushes. My camera clicked away, primed with a new SD card. My others were now safely lodged in the flat in Manaus.

Although it was only two weeks or so since we stopped here, the inlet he was looking for eluded him for some time, such is the growth of the plant life here. Once found, we hacked the entrance clear and, using paddles, found our way to a clearing. We jumped ashore and carried what was necessary for an overnight stop, away from the water and its inherent dangers. We rigged up the tent we now carried for this second expedition, under the trees. It looked a lot more comfortable than the boat. As before, the clearing had a low count of pests because of a species of lianas that covered the trees in the area. With my help, José set up the fire and generally saw that everything was in order. It was still light and he suggested he went alone into the town this time round, to replenish the bread and anything else we might need before the next stop. He obviously thought I was capable of staying on my own. I was a little taken aback despite his obvious confidence in my ability to stay on my own.

'There is not much point in both of us going,' he said. 'I can get all that we want. I hoped you would stay here and look after our camp.' I could hardly refuse, put that way. It meant he trusted me implicitly. He looked questioningly at me at his suggestion and I nodded and smiled. He seemed satisfied with my confident answer and got ready to leave. He smartened himself up prior to leaving and I was a little surprised at that too.

'You have your rifle and I'll be as quick as I can,' he said as he cast off.

I added wood to the fire he'd started until it was burning away merrily. I heaped on plenty more wood and went off, carrying the fishing line to the bank of the inlet. I took out the Swiss Army Knife fastened on the inside of my belt. It reminded me of when I first saw it among my father's effects. It was that which triggered my first urge to travel to Manaus and what has followed. It would be the first time I had used it since coming here. I flipped out a round, pointed blade, probably for taking out stones from horses' hooves. I gouged under the bark of the nearest tree and soon found a grub for my purpose. A few minutes after casting it into water on the hook of the fishing line I felt the line tighten and hauled in a fish of some sort. I speared it through the neck with the main blade of the penknife till it ceased to wriggle. It looked similar to one I had eaten on a previous occasion. It was adequate for the two of us, so I packed away the line. Remembering José's words of warning however, I held it down with my foot and cut off its head. Following his example, I cut off the tail and got rid of the innards. These were all thrown back into the stream. I washed the prepared carcase and tied it into a plastic bag before any unseen, watching creature got ideas. I didn't fancy cooking it till José came back as it should be eaten fresh. After an hour or so I became a little worried about his absence. The ease with which he had left still puzzled me a little. The unease nagged at me. What if he didn't return at all, what would I do? I couldn't continue alone; when should I return to Manaus? It was the first time I'd been alone at night without him. I started to panic, almost as a child waking up in the dark and calling out for a parent. I thought about my father and how he had done our previous journey on his own with only native bearers. The thought of his bravery gave me the courage to stop being a coward. I stoked up the fire and opened a tin of biscuits and a bottle of beer. I cursed José for not being back and went to bed.

It was quite late when he returned and I heard him singing a Portuguese pop song that was on the local radio quite a lot. He was some way off and the sound travelled across the water as all the sounds do here. He had trouble mooring the boat on his own in the blackness, and I could hear him muttering and swearing; mostly in his own tongue. I pretended not to hear him and left him to struggle, *serves him right*. When he finally appeared and made his way over to the fire, I feigned sleep, and eventually he decided to wake me.

I detected the smell of beer and he slurred his words. Fair enough, I thought. He'd taken advantage of the opportunity to call in some tavern for a few beers after shopping. But I whiffed a hint of perfume and there was an added air of satisfaction that was obvious. Aiparuca would be a port of call on some of his excursion trips and he'd know knew where to find a lady for the night. The rich tourists would be escorted to a hotel in town and he would find a bar and some of his own countrymen.

I made no comment but I was a bit annoyed not to have been invited to accompany him and have the same opportunity. This was a serious expedition we were embarking on and I was a little annoyed at his going for a night out at the first opportunity. On the other hand I think I would have been out of my depth with a Portuguese-speaking female. I couldn't blame him; it was just sour grapes. He'd only had my company for the past fortnight. My sense of humour rose to the surface and I imagined myself a neglected wife in a sit-com.

'And where the hell have you been till now? You've been with another woman haven't you? I can smell her perfume, so don't lie

to me. My mother was right. I should have never married you in the first place. I smiled to myself at the thought and simply said:

'Did you get any rumpty-pumpty, José?' He looked at me, puzzled, and noticed my smile in the firelight, but didn't bite.

'I got some nice crisp baguettes we both like, Martin.' He smiled, 'and of course a case of that beer we both like.' I didn't reply, I simply threw some fresh dry logs on the fire and it was soon blazing away again. He sensed my pique and remained silent. *I'm behaving silly.*

'I caught a nice fish, José, but it's too dark now to collect vegetables to go with it.' I fetched the fish and showed it to him. It looked a little limp in its plastic bag. 'I'll get rid of it.' And without more ado, I took it over to the river, emptied it out and returned to the fireside. I didn't tell him about my biscuits and beer.

'I fancy one of those baguettes with some cheese, José. And a bottle of that beer would go down well with it; I'm thirsty as Hell. I think it's sitting by this fire all night.' My words got through to him and he was suitably chastened. I remained by the fire and he prepared the bread and cheese and came and sat beside me with a couple of the beers. He had had time to think about my remarks and sobered up a little. He now knew why I was silent. To break it, he described the town and sheepishly tried to explain his lateness. 'I have sometimes called there before,' he began.

'There are some shops and a bar on the edge of town and it's much cheaper than the main shopping centre. I met a friend that used to live in my apartment block in Manaus. He has moved to Aiparuca and now works in the small supermarket there. He is manager of the shop and it is where

I bought all the groceries. He was proud of how things had gone for him since he left Manaus. He has a flat above the shop. As it was near closing time, he invited me to meet his new wife. She also works in the supermarket. He insisted on me staying for a meal with them. We talked and talked and I had several beers and forgot about the time. I'm sorry Martin, but I had not seen him for a long time.'

It could have been true so I passed it off and hoped he enjoyed it. I asked to tell me more about this old friend, hoping to catch him out, but it all sounded plausible. I resolved not to adopt that attitude in future. He could do as he liked and I am not my brother's keeper.

I don't think he suspected my first thoughts of why he was late, but he never asked me what rumpty-pumpty was. We enjoyed the late meal and I suggested a nightcap for us both from one of the bottles of brandy I'd purchased as an alternative to his home brew. They were liberal measures and we finished up singing songs. The first would be in Portuguese and the next in English, each of us teaching the other the words. It was something we'd done before when in a mellow mood at night. On these occasions and in a clearing it was magical. If there were no rain, the sky above would have been filled with more stars than I'd ever seen in England. We would sing louder and louder, sometimes together. None of the neighbours complained.

My irritation was forgotten the next morning. I don't think he could have made up such a story in the state he was in.

I thought I was now used to the weather in the rainforest, but as we began the second section of our journey it became worse. First time around we had encountered the *Arquipélago*

175

das Anavilhana in a northeasterly direction. It had been a pleasant detour with a microcosm of colourful birds and butterflies and the weather had been kind. This time José's plan was to avoid it by keeping to the west fork of the Rio Negro calling at Novo Airão and then Aruja. The reason was to show me different aspects of the rainforest. Unfortunately, the rain was monsoonal and pretty soon we were wet despite the canopy of the boat. It was as if the river was rising as we watched it. Pretty soon, thick saplings and huge branches from trees were swirling towards us. I took up a position at the front and did my best to divert large debris from smashing into the boat. The current was moving faster because of the extra water and José had difficulty controlling it. It was almost like shooting rapids. Several times José thought it wiser to shelter in some inlet to avoid floating branches. The torrent took its toll on the wildlife too. Turtles and other river life were being swept out of control in the broiling waters and were hurled into rocks on the banks.

José philosophised about the situation, saying time was not of the essence and suggested it would be better if we found shelter and made camp. The floodwaters had encroached into the forest and we floated between trees away from the river proper. I could tell from his expression that this wasn't an ideal spot to make camp, but it was better the Devil you know. By now pinpointing our whereabouts had become difficult for him. There was no sun and all recognised landmarks had been swept away. He was losing track of his bearings due to the overcast sky. I could tell by his expression that despite his years of battling these conditions, even he was having difficulty. At his signal, we got out of the boat and tied it between two trees that had petrified in the past and had no foliage. It lessened the odds of being invaded during the night by creatures seeking shelter from the elements. Fishing was out of the question so we had to resort to emergency rations for a change: biscuits and tinned meat. A hot drink was impossible, so a brandy and water had to suffice. There was no way we could light a fire and even using the primus stove could have been dodgy. The rain was still raging so we ate the food, José lit his cigar and we got a little drunk with more brandy. We reminisced about our respective younger days in an effort to ignore the storm and pass the time. Time dragged with no let-up in the torrential rain. It was still early but José suggested we try to get some sleep and if it cleared up during the night we would set off at first light.

I think we both woke up together. We'd slept well because of the brandy but the boat was rocking violently from side to side and tilting from end to end at an alarming angle. The rain had stopped and in a few short hours the waters had receded fast. We both realised at the same time what had happened. The boat was swinging clear of the trees because it was anchored to two of them, and the ropes were of a different length. It was something we hadn't thought about. In our hammocks we were swinging like the boat, but OK, some of our equipment and stores were now on the boggy ground around. We retrieved most of it after untying the ropes. We sank into the mire up to our knees in the process. The boat was now in a quagmire of forest undergrowth. We knew what we had to do without a discussion. With the front rope over our shoulders we hauled the floundered craft back towards the river. José, of course, was leading and hoped to find deep water to float away quickly from here. The sun had scarcely risen, but the glimmer of it was enough for him to work out in which direction we had to haul the boat to the safety of the river. Even so, the boat would catch on stumps and other debris, and it was an hour before it slid satisfyingly into deep enough water to make it buoyant of its own accord. We climbed aboard and using the oars paddled our way into the river proper. At the first decent mooring place we pulled in and secured the boat, assessing the damage. After tidying up we made an inventory and discovered nothing of importance was missing. Unfortunately water had got into the outboard motor and I was glad I had a little knowledge to eventually get it dried out and fired up. By now the sun was up and the rain had abated altogether. José found a reasonable inlet that had dry land each side. By this time we were fairly exhausted.

'Let us rest here for a couple of hours,' he said. 'We will have some food and then think about going on our way. That was certainly an episode for your diary, Martin, and one to recount to your friends when you get back. It's the sort of thing that can happen here at any time but it is the worst I have ever known. You did very well and I am glad I was not alone. I know very little about engines and it would have been worse for me without you.' It was said quietly and I was pleased he saw me as an equal part of the team. I must have swelled with the compliment and grinned.

'Like you, I must have inherited my skills of survival from our father, and I don't mean God. He gave one of his genuine loud laughs.

Chapter 15

My rifle had survived the episode but had water in the barrel and chamber. I cleaned it, checked the box of cartridges and fired a shot into a tree; it was in good order. I tossed a line into the tributary to catch a fish where we were moored. José sorted out some food and got the spirit stove going. Ten minutes went by without any success on my part to catch a fish. This was unusual, normally all the waters were teeming with fish. José said not to bother.

'It is probably for the best,' he said. 'Sometimes the water in these channels is so acidic from certain vegetation that that the fish avoid them. Those that survive can cause an upset stomach.' I was learning that nothing can be taken for granted where the rainforests are concerned.

Disappointed, I said, 'then why don't I shoot a small mammal as you agreed I could, Jose?' I said it questioningly like a small boy. I'd been itching to show off my skill. He pointed to the clearing.

'All right,' he conceded, 'but we must keep very quiet. I think you should rest your rifle on the edge of the boat and keep your head down. If I see a possible animal that is eatable

I will signal to you.' He took some biscuits and broke them into pieces. Walking to the far end of the clearing, he placed them beside a small pool of water and returned. We remained motionless, me prone with the rifle resting on the edge of the boat. José crouched behind me, 'for safety,' he said with his usual smile. We hadn't long to wait. A squirrel monkey edged its way down a tree and, looking round all the time, started towards the bait.

José touched me on the shoulder and shook his head. I had visions that the plan would fail and the biscuits would disappear into the canopy one by one, eaten by the uneatable. My idea had been so simple when I bought the gun. I hadn't reckoned with the wildlife. Then I noticed a movement in the dead leaves surrounding the pool. A small rodent surfaced and sniffed the smaller crumbs left by the squirrel monkey. It saw the monkey leaving and grabbed a mouthful of the crumbs. I had a bead on it and fired even though I hadn't had conformation from behind. The monkey flew back up the tree at the sound and the small beast did a somersault and lay twitching. Before I could say a word, José had jumped over the side and raced across the clearing. He returned holding the rodent by its tail jubilantly. It was still jerking in its death throes so he whirled it round a couple of times and hit its head against the nearest tree. He laid it on the floor beside me to inspect. It looked like a brown rat to me. José said it was a half grown Agouti. It was about the size of a small rabbit and was edible but tough. He set about preparing it. In his usual no-nonsense way he reached for his sharp all-purpose machete and, using a fallen log well away from the boat, removed its head, legs, skin and innards. He left these on his makeshift chopping board and returned to the boat. Before he had cooked the flesh, the offal had disappeared in all directions. I had a field day with my camera, adding a marmoset, several howlers and a bird of prey that I couldn't identify. Countless rats were in attendance and squabbles went on until the last of the Agouti's remains disappeared. The memory of the rats lingered when I tried to sleep that night.

'We must do this more often,' I said as we threw the remains over the side of the boat after eating all we needed from the cooked meat. That's one thing I like about this place. There's no need for refuse collectors, wheelie bins and the effect on the environment.

It was late afternoon by now and despite the rain that still persisted on and off, the atmosphere was generally warm. José said it was better if we didn't push on. We'd had a rough twenty-four hours and come out of it in one piece. I was glad of his suggestion. We'd agreed from the start that there was no urgency to our mission. Let the elements do their worst and when they'd had their fun, we would resume at our convenience.

'After what has happened these last two days I think we should have a change of plan,' he said. 'These floods will be general and it will be difficult to take the route to Novo Airão and Aruja.' He showed me the map. 'Eventually we would have had to head northeast overland anyway if we wish to enter the Terra Indigena Waimiri Atroari reservation, and that is our destination. It will be much better to keep the boat to the right hand bank and head for a place called Aldeia Vila Batista. A few kilometres before we reach there, we will look for a tributary that will take us further towards our destination.

Smaller inlets will branch off and we shall continue using them till one of them becomes too shallow to proceed further. At least the rains have let us make more use of the boat. Then it will be forest only and the rest of the journey will be on foot. We will haul the boat into the forest and hide it safely till our return. After that we shall continue on foot to the southern end of the reserve. This will be the most difficult part of the journey. We have to cut our way with machetes as we did when finding the Nucutanis. It is all unknown territory for me and we will have to mark our path very carefully for the return journey.

'An easier route would, of course, be to go by way of Aldeia Vila, as the waterways are much wider. But there is a danger of being spotted by tours on the other side of the town. The war-like tribes I have heard about are also on the lookout for innocent travellers unaccompanied in that area. The way I have indicated is more difficult but we are less likely to be observed by anyone, friend or foe. We will be also be approaching from the direction they are not expecting tourists. We will have that advantage, Martin. Are you willing to try it? It is also the way I think our father went from things I see on the photos.' My wry smile and nod told him I had no opinion when it came to his forest know-how. I trusted him implicitly; there was no need for my input. How he explained it was good enough for me and he nodded. He hadn't spelled out the dangers; he didn't need to.

I had read enough to know that there are still headhunters in the heart of some of these reserves. The captured victims are beheaded and the fleshy part of the skull is removed. The skin is then replaced and shrunk. The perpetrator wears the end product on his waistband.

There are fifteen thousand square kilometres of jungle for them to hide in. These tribes have lived in isolation from each other for so long that their practices have gone to extremes by virtue of good and evil leaders. Sacrifices are the norm in some tribes. The initiation ceremonies I saw by the Nucutanis are mild in comparison to this tribe José had heard about from the elders. He no longer skirted round the possible dangers. I had survived this last episode, and he was giving me an opportunity to say enough was enough, let's go back. In other words, things could get worse.

There was no doubt that each day that passed now, made our visit to the Nucutanis seem like a holiday jaunt. I was under no illusions. During the few weeks I had been in José's company I had gradually got the picture. The urges and excitement I felt, when I first saw those black and white images paled in comparison to what I was experiencing in reality. What I'd discovered with the help of José had made me part of it. I couldn't back out now, whatever the consequences. Had I known what I would have had to endure before I set out from Cornwall, I would now be sunbathing in some Mediterranean resort. I only hope I live to return there one day.

Chapter 16

Things went more or less in the way I'd come to expect after my experiences so far with José. It was never easy and never the same. Every waterway had new problems. Most of them had changed since José had previously travelled that way. Fresh dangers rose unexpectedly. I saw my first crocodile as we prepared to pull in for a break.

We'd had to resort to paddles. José seemed to have a sixth sense about what lay beneath and would test the depth of the water and swing the outboard motor out of it. He would hand me a paddle and we would manoeuvre the craft into deeper water. On this occasion even he was not ready for the new danger. I was at the front of the boat and as he steered towards a landing area I saw the snout peeping over the bank. I shouted and pointed at the same time. He reacted quickly and as we cleared the bank, half a dozen of the crocodile's friends waddled slowly towards us in a threatening manner. José said that it wasn't as if they would attack us, but any movement in the waters of their territory set them looking for food. There was no limit to the size of their prey and, once they had made short work of it and consumed it, they rested.

To me it was a near miss but to José it was a non-event. It was something that occurred sometimes and not even life-threatening. These reptiles have existed for millions of years and they have a simple philosophy. They wait for the opportunity and strike. If victims avoid them they shrug their scaly shoulders and wait. They manage without food for long periods and when a victim falls prey to them, they gorge themselves. They never worry about being attacked; they are the top dog predators. That's why they have been here forever.

My heart thumped for some time after. He could see I had paled beneath my new tan and he laughed. I placed his hand on my heart.

'The last time that happened,' I said, 'was just before I left Britain.'

'And what caused this excitement?' he said, puzzled. I told him about Ella and my first time with her. 'And what about those two Brazilian beauties in the hotel,' he went on.

'Not the same thing,' I said, 'anyway I was pissed on a hundred percent white rum.' He explained about the crocs.

'We would have served them well. After swallowing us in large chunks they would have rested for several days till we were digested. The way they waddled, perhaps we were lucky and they weren't hungry.' His remarks didn't make me feel any safer. I wondered how long it would be before I lost my twitchiness about the unknown dangers that waited round every corner, so to speak.

Apart from my nervousness regarding fearsome creatures I tended to forget them as my camera clicked continuously at all the new species that seemed almost eager for me to snap them. I was spoilt for numbers and variety. José pointed out a capybara hiding at the edge of the river under vegetation. I can hardly believe it's a rodent. They are very shy and quite harmless. This one was like a brown Billy Bunter, round and as heavy as a man. With short legs and ears and hardly any tail it seemed to float away as we approached. Not much of a picture to capture. During that day a manatee surfaced almost under the boat as the motor disturbed it, another ugly brute with no camera aspirations. The first time I saw one, it was as if I had disturbed a fat naked bather, quite human-like for a second. They are quite harmless. However, I never tired of the clouds of butterflies, always a different colour than the last. Conversely, all the other flying insects were to be avoided. I never got used to the flying pests that followed us and greeted us at every turn. I swear they could smell our sweat from a mile away. In the forest I had learned to be aware each time I put a foot down. I learned never to place a hand anywhere without looking first. Ants, centipedes, scorpions, and countless others were waiting take a stab at you. In the air hornets, wasps and even bees, which in England are benign unless threatened, had to be avoided as they zoomed past in every direction, attacking just for the fun of it. I thought of the Nucutanis. Darwin's natural selection must apply to them. Over the centuries they had become impervious to their hostile surroundings. On the other hand, they could be wiped out by common infections from strangers they came in contact with.

I recalled other strange sights during my stay with the Nucutanis. In the short time I was there, I had seen a baby being suckled by a bitch. Young men with fresh scars from initiation ceremonies going about their business, ignoring the flies stuck to them, as if they were non-existent. Children would make a game of swatting hornets and the like. One picked up a scorpion as I watched and smashed its head against a rock. The child would probably eat it later. I suddenly realised that I must be getting used to this way of life if my thoughts could wander about recalling such events.

José had secured the boat at what looked a safe haven and we stopped for lunch. We ventured into the edge of the clearing and found fruit in the form of green figs. On these food-gathering trips José used a bag with a strap that looped across his shoulder. It had several pockets, each with a flap fastened with Velcro. He kept the items we collected separate till we got back. We added cassava roots, a potato-like tuber. This was a source of starch and would be mashed up. He added some dry leaves from a bush, probably some herb for taste to his recipes. The ubiquitous Brazil nut tree provided another ingredient to our diet. Even that surprised me. The large nut is actually a seed and as many as two-dozen nuts are contained in the actual shell. On the way back, José spotted a cinchona tree. It's known as the fever bark tree. The dark, bitter bark is rich in quinine and I was now used to sampling the horrible syrup that José enjoyed giving me daily. It prevents malaria, he says, and I have learned to accept his judgment in all things. I'm lucky to have such a knowledgeable pharmacist to administer to my needs, although he probably gets a kick out of my discomfort, like any older brother.

Chapter 17

We have several more days of similar negotiations of narrow waterways. The humidity never lets up. In between, the heavy rains suddenly make us take cover. José simply sits there or if it is a prolonged downpour he'll smoke a cigar. I wish I had his stoicism. As I watch him serenely puffing and now and then blowing a perfect ring in the safety of the canvas canopy I wish I smoked, at least for this trip. I'd never tried it. Health warnings were enough of a deterrent. At university I never felt the need to calm my nerves while studying. I once tried a couple of puffs from a fellow student's *joint*, or a *spliff* as he called it. It was pleasant enough but had no more effect than a pint of lager.

The waterways were now quite narrow. Thankfully, so is the boat and apart from hacking overgrown greenery, we forged on. The scenery gets monotonous on our evening lay-ups and I stare into the gloom. There is little wildlife to break the tedium and my camera stays in its case, within its waterproof bag. The screeching of the monkeys and birds seems more plaintive. They must be bored too. I get a little despondent with these inactive periods. I'm sure José noticed it. He'd make conversation but it didn't help. I felt sweat trickle down my neck and a large mosquito headed towards me after taking one sniff from José's cigar. I swore as I swiped at it with a length of fern, missed and cracked my wrist against a canopy upright. José couldn't stand it any longer. He came over. In his hand he had one of the pipes I'd seen being smoked by one or two of the Nucutani men at the knees-up. They were fashioned out of the shell of a large nut. The base had been pierced and a length of thin, hollow bamboo inserted.

'It was one given to me by Tunaku and has never been used.' He reached into his collecting satchel and took out a handful of the dried leaves. He crushed a few of them and filled the bowl. Handed it to me stem first.

'Try it, Martin, no harm will come to you I swear.'

I placed it in my mouth and sucked. All I could detect was green bamboo. He struck a match and held it out. I took it and placed the flame into the bowl. Smoke arose and then I tasted fumes from the leaves. I inhaled and a flavour like cough medicine hit the back of my throat. It was not unpleasant and not as acrid as I would have thought it would be. It certainly wasn't pot. I trusted José and smoked it for several minutes. I didn't inhale every time I took a puff. Nothing startling happened. I tapped the ashes into the water and handed it back.

'Not much of a kick in it, José.' I said. I lay back and noticed that the mosquitoes were less noisy. The howlers had stopped howling and the sweat had stopped trickling down my back. I dozed off. Havuana was beckoning me and I followed her into a hut. We made love and when we both climaxed I looked into her face and it was Ella. She pushed me away, laughing. When I woke from this dream it was dark. José was standing over me.

'Wasn't that much better than watching the rain, Martin? By the smile on your face, you seem to have been enjoying yourself.'

'I must have dozed off for a few minutes,' I replied. 'It must have been that pipe. What was in it?'

'You have been asleep for four hours, my friend. Do you feel good?' I admitted that I felt great. 'Then you must smoke your pipe when I have my cigar at night if you feel a little down.' I asked him again what was in it.

'I'm sure I could trust you if I told you, Martin, but I am sworn to secrecy. The Indians of the forest have been exploited for over two centuries. First they were captured to work as slaves and turned out of the land that belonged to them. Only recently, gold was discovered in one of the reservations and prospectors have come from far and wide invading the village and attacking the people. If the leaves Tunaku and the others smoke were discovered, they would be invaded. I love them too much to risk that. I trust you, Martin, but you may risk telling a friend in a pub after a couple of pints when you go back home, and the secret would be out.'

I understood and was content to smoke the pipe when I'd had a bad day.

We did have brighter moments, of course. Nature would surprise us with an oasis. We never waited till it got dark before stopping. One of us would spot a shaft of sunlight through the darkness and we'd investigate. If we were lucky, a clearing would emerge and the sun beamed down on it. Usually these clearings were the result of poachers who had found a stand of rare trees, walnut and the like. It was always unexpected and we didn't think twice when they appeared. We would smile at each other and, whatever time of the day we saw one of these paradises, we took advantage of them, abandoning our expedition into the unknown.

It was a reward that we couldn't resist and it spurred us on afterwards. We were self-sufficient and no one was awaiting our return. We intended to enjoy these opportunities when they presented themselves. After a few more days I could see it was completely new territory even to José and he admitted it.

He had a general map of the rivers and some of the tributaries, but the latter changed almost daily, he said. He had a compass and he relied heavily on the sun and stars when they were available. With what little I'd learned, I sensed we didn't always go in a straight line and thought I'd seen a particular tree before on the bank. I didn't comment. There were no signposts and my newfound brother relied on experience and instinct. Once, the narrow channel widened out and he looked perplexed. He stopped the boat and listened. We both heard the sound of rushing water. It was an unexpected small section of white-water rapids through rocks that we saw in time. The boat could have been smashed. We pulled into the bank and tied up. He went ashore and returned having found a route for us to detour the danger. He pointed through the undergrowth and we entered a flooded forest area. We manually hauled the boat between trees hoping to find a passage around the problem.

Luck was with us again. We found an oasis of a different kind. The ground was raised quite high and clear of the surrounding forest. This was in complete contrast to subsidence that had fashioned the rapids we'd just avoided. We came to the conclusion that some huge underground catastrophe had changed the terrain in this fashion. Perhaps a meteorite had caused it. Whatever it was had been powerful enough to have twisted the ground in such a way, but we were thankful.

We rested the craft and surveyed the plateau, for that's what it was. It was about half the size of a football pitch and roughly oval in shape. It sloped slightly upwards away from us and midway was a fresh water pool fed from an underground spring that bubbled clear water and made its way towards us into the tributary we had just left. The pool was ten feet across and roughly circular. There were no large animals in attendance for some reason; a few small ones that had been there fled as we approached. The spring was quite exposed and the daring ones knew they were easy targets from above and below. It was an ideal spot for their predators. The evidence of this was the small bleached bones that lay around. The water was crystal clear except for animal droppings around the edge. I asked José why the clearing wasn't overgrown with vegetation.

'Countless animals of all description would use this waterhole despite the risks. Until a predator strikes it would become crowded. Very quickly they would lose that sense of fear they are born with and graze on the vegetation that is readily available near the pool. Like us they have discovered paradise and threw caution to the wind. At the same time, they are keeping it tidy like a lawn mower. Then one or two will become careless and down swoops an eagle for a rodent.

Maybe a puma or a jaguar will pounce on a deer. The ones that escape with their little hearts thumping will take a long time before they return here again; but they will, and so it goes on, Martin. Some of these bones are only a week or so old. When we arrived there were already a few daring ones risking the same fate for a drink.' I asked how safe it was for us. He scooped up a handful of water and smelled it. He tasted it and then filled a water bottle.

'It is safe to drink,' he said assuredly. 'You should know that the animals would not be drinking here if it was poisonous.' He laughed. 'It is not difficult to be a forest smart-arse is it?' Smart-arse was one of the words he had picked up from me and he liked using them, 'but if you are thinking of bathing without your clothes on you must be aware of something. I have seen footprints of a large cat around the edges.' He laughed. 'They could be of that elusive jaguar that you were hoping to see. Your bare arse would certainly make him lick his lips.' I couldn't tell if he was joking or not, so I suggested a compromise. 'You stand guard with my rifle and I'll go in with my clothes on?' I ventured. He agreed and we both enjoyed the cool water in turn, the other keeping guard.

Refreshed, we took the rest of the day off and, without effort, prepared our evening meal. We foraged for suitable fruit and veg in the forest close to our mooring. We moved silently through the trees as we did so and with a tap on the shoulder José pointed to a small squirrel. I missed it with my first shot but there was so much noise in the treetops it was unaware and carried on eating its nut. I scored a bull's eye with my next and it toppled to the ground. I raced over and fetched it like any self-respecting gun dog, before a thieving monkey took it into the canopy.

José fixed up a fire in the clearing and spit-roasted it after getting rid of the offal in the usual way. The meal was delicious and we rounded it off with a couple of my brandies. Because of the proximity to the water-hole, we securely fixed the canvas sheeting around the boat. I felt good and we talked for a while before turning in. I didn't need a pipe of pleasant dreams that night.

Chapter 18

I slept well and the light filtering from the clearing seemed a good omen. José's unusual silence over breakfast told me that he had something on his mind. We carried out our ablutions and tidied up ready for another day's trekking. I felt fit enough to tackle anything the forest would throw at us after our day of rest.

We'd hauled the boat past the rocky rapids that had caused us to pull in here yesterday and were about to launch it back onto smoother waters. He stopped and looked at me.

'I think today is the day when we will have to abandon the boat and make our way through the forest on foot. I have an idea it will take us several days to reach our goal with luck. Then we should be somewhere near the tribe where I think William Lockwood took those pictures that have so far mystified me. We are doing well, Martin, are you ready for the going to get more difficult?'

I nodded in all seriousness.

'I can't give up now, José, I owe that much to my father's memory. I had so little regard for him when he was alive, and my guilt never seems to go away. Whatever I do will not match up to what he did single-handed.'

He didn't question my answer and the boat slid into the water as we pushed.

Very soon it was obvious to me that there was too little draft for comfort. The water was narrowing too. We were drawing towards the source of this tributary. At a signal from José, we dragged the reluctant vessel onto a convenient clearing. I stayed with it and José went into the forest searching for a route to begin our journey on foot. It was an hour before he returned and his efforts showed on his sweat-stained clothes. He looked at his compass, glanced at the sun and sat down.

'I have found a clearing created by a fire. It will take us about twenty minutes to reach. It looks like a convenient spot for our starting point. I climbed a tree and could see the ground rising in the distance slightly. I think this is the beginning of the Terra Indigena Waimiri Atroari. I have had such a view before on tours and it compares with maps I have studied. First we must hide the boat as far as possible into the forest. Well away from even this trickle. You know by now that in a few days this could become flooded.'

We struggled for more than an hour to find a suitable spot that satisfied José and removed all that was necessary to carry in our backpacks for what lay ahead. We both checked and agreed we'd left nothing that we might need before returning here.

After securing it in a thicket of small trees we covered it in branches till it was almost invisible. I could see leaving it there was a wrench. I knew what the boat meant to him.

'What if we can't find it?' I said, smiling, to lighten the moment. He saw the funny side and laughed, his normal laugh. We went around the perimeter of the hiding place. Using the machetes that would be doing their stuff for the next day or two, we marked some substantial trees with an X on all sides for several yards. We left nothing to chance. From whichever direction we returned we should locate it. When José was satisfied we set off in the direction he had reconnoitred for an hour. He had already marked the way and cleared it ready. In twenty minutes as he said, we arrived at the clearing. From then on, our tree markings became a routine task. The rainforest is vast, and we intended to find our way back to his precious boat, come what may.

We toiled for the rest of the day hacking away at the undergrowth but at the same time treading our way carefully. We rested for five minutes every quarter of an hour. This gave us a breather and in the silence we peered forward in case of possible danger. Before setting out again and with my help, José would climb a suitable tree and, using a small telescope, he would reassess the direction we should take on resuming our journey. Sometimes this would require a rope and my assistance and we would ascend until we had a view of the distant canopies. As we climbed, the monkeys would make aggressive noises thinking we were intruders, but backed away at the same time.

'Perhaps they think you are going to rape their wives,' said José.

'Without the hospitality I received from Tunaku's people, I might have thought about it,' I laughed.

We enjoyed these diversions. There would be gaps in the panorama of the forest and we caught glimpses of rivers from our bird's eye view that were spectacular. José made new sketches each time, leaving nothing to chance. He showed them to me each time, adding, 'in case, Martin.' I understood why he did this. In this un-chartered landscape there was danger lurking, and we could be separated. He was thinking of my welfare. It was a sobering thought and reminded me to take the expedition seriously. He was quite pleased with our progress. The weather had been kind and, apart from the usual sweating, it wasn't too bad. He suggested we stop well before darkness again. 'We could quickly lose our bearings otherwise.'

This enabled us to find a suitable campsite while it was light. We would look for a tree with a fork well off the ground, yet still not high enough for the howlers and their friends to interfere with us during the night. One good thing about the canopy dwellers is that they very rarely come down to ground level. They were safe from predators up there. In addition and to be on the safe side, we fashioned a shelf roughly six foot by four foot out of branches over our makeshift bedroom. Each time we came across such hazards I thought of my father with only native non-English speaking guides. He was now Superman in my eyes. We both carried a waterproof. One was for us to lie on and the other went over us. It had a double purpose of course. One to keep off the rain and the other any intruders, we hoped.

When José was satisfied with its construction, we left it and lit a fire in the clearing. Then we ate food that we had collected during the day. We even sat and chatted afterwards, he with his cigar and me with my pipe – I would definitely need it tonight. By now he showed me which plant I needed for the tobacco, so I collected my own. He knew the secret was safe with me. There was a certain satisfaction about collecting all this free bounty that nature had to offer.

We climbed the tree and tied ourselves in. It wasn't the best night's sleep but it served its purpose. We both woke up several times during the night as if on sentry duty. I didn't feel particularly refreshed in the morning. I just hoped that I didn't have too many such uncomfortable nights in the future.

The second day was more arduous. In addition to heavy rain we also encountered other obstacles. Huge trees would bar our path, felled by storms or subsidence. Craters would appear, some so deep we needed to go round them, adding to my frustration. Each time we veered from a straight line, out would come our marker pens in the form of the machetes. Crosses carved in the trees would be our salvation on the return journey. Every time we stopped, we sharpened the machetes on a whetstone for the purpose. José said there was not much point in stopping early today as we were already wet through from rain on the outside and sweat on the inside of our clothes. He spurred me on by intimating that he felt we would reach our goal today if we pushed on. I believed him and doggedly drove myself on. Just when I thought I would have to rebel, he called a halt. I think he read my thoughts.

He, of course, had enough energy to climb a tree before the darkness fell in. I offered to help but he shrugged it off. I watched him as he struggled to the top branch and looked around. I saw his gaze stop in one direction and then he descended.

His broad smile said it all. *'It is better than I thought. Luck has smiled on us at last. Martin, there is a large clearing and much smoke and many people,'* he said, as if he were Tonto and I was the Lone Ranger. He didn't quite understand my loud laugh at his remark and I didn't enlighten him. He gripped my hand with his elation and hugged me; despite the smell I enjoyed it. He was proud of me even though he didn't say so. We repeated the previous night's preparations for a tree-house and I had little trouble sleeping on this occasion even without a pipe. The arduous journey was over, or so I misguidedly thought. In reality it hadn't even begun.

Chapter 19

Although inwardly we were both excited, even apprehensive about today, we went about our routine calmly. We checked our equipment and marked our territory like some rutting stag or randy tomcat. This was our return point, said José, and stressed that should things go wrong I was to make for here whatever. He had drawn a map, his own map, detailing every step of the way so far. He gave it to me and asked if I understood it. When we had scarred the trees, he had impressed on me the type of tree it was. He had taught me about the sun and the main stars at night. At the time I had thought it was to pass the time away on dark nights. Now I realised it was in the event of something happening to him and I had to return alone. He was taking all these precautions for my benefit. The back of my neck went cold as this sunk in.

'Don't be afraid my little brother, I know you can do it. I have watched you.' He gripped my shoulder and looked into my face. 'Don't worry, we shall return together. I am sure more than ever now that where we go tomorrow is where our father went. I am amazed at his bravery and it is why we must try at least to go where he dared. You have endured all the hardships he experienced and now come the dangers he risked so long ago. We should see these people in a few hours and then you can take pictures of them from a distance. There is no way we should try to make friends with them. William Lockwood did and returned unscathed, except for the scar on his arm. Maybe he was lucky. Maybe at that time they had a gentle leader when he called. I don't think we should take that chance. If they are the war-like tribe I have heard about in the last few years, it will be better to return to Manaus before they spot us. We will not be welcome except for their evil pleasures. It will be enough that we have found them.'

José went in front as usual and insisted that I keep well behind. My safety was very much on his mind. like the older brother that he had become in both our minds. We went at a much slower pace and he examined the trees and the ground carefully for any telltale signs of these people. As the indications became numerous I felt a tenseness in the back of my neck with each few steps. There could be traps also. An innocent trailing vine could come to life and leave the victim dangling in the air. A sharpened bamboo stake could strike from the trees. José had explained all these things to me before we ventured forward. All these traps were set by the hunters, not only for us but also for unsuspecting animals. The Nucutanis did all these things around their territory for the same reason.

Normally José would remark about things as we passed them, but not today. He was concentrating our safety and determined not to be taken by surprise; more for my sake I think. He felt he had the responsibility of an older brother.

There were gaps through the canopy caused by the tribe's continuous use of the surrounds of their village and the overhead sun was at its hottest. We stopped for something to eat and it gave us a respite from our nervousness. No fire of course. We had gathered fruit and nuts on the way and sat in the shade of a huge tree. As we ate, we both commented on the increased amount of footprints as we progressed. These were not stray ones. 'We are getting very close to these people,' he whispered.

'There is still no proper trail or well-trodden path yet,' he added, 'but we shall see one soon.'

Another hour and more sunlight was filtering through the canopy. Now I could see signs of children's footprints too and my excitement was almost unbearable. José stopped, turned and beckoned me towards him and then motioned for me to tread even more carefully, without breaking even the smallest twig underfoot. As I reached his shoulder, he pointed through to clear sky through a purpose-built tunnel in the undergrowth. There would be several of these, kept clear around the village. They would help villagers keep a sense of direction when they went out and returned. We edged forward, closer to the exit. José indicated for me to follow him into the trees at the side, away from the main well-worn path. He didn't want a villager discovering us. We moved several yards through the thicket until we were well hidden. We peered through the leaves of a bush and finally saw the village before us. The sight was unbelievable.

An enormous clearing disappeared into the distance, rising up a gentle slope as it did, in keeping with the river. It was a huge pear-drop in shape and was an island dividing the river that ran at each side of it. From our viewpoint it started in the northeast and slanted across and to our left, that is the southwest. José took out his telescope and moved forward, placing it in a gap but without it protruding, to get a more detailed view. I remained in the shadow of the overhanging branches behind him. Then, cupping his hand over the end to prevent reflection, he moved the instrument from left to right over the whole scene. When he was satisfied he had seen enough, he lowered it and retreated to my position, then beckoned me to silently follow him back to a safer position. We didn't stop till we were well back into the woods, away from any sign of footprints.

'And is it them?' I asked anxiously.

'I'm pretty sure,' he replied.

'Nature has found them a good spot,' I offered.

'Nature has nothing to do with it,' came the reply. We sat down and he cleared the forest floor at our feet. He drew a map with a stick of what he had seen with the telescope and his opinion of what he had construed from it.

'They are the Winukanatu tribe; of that I am sure, Martin,' he began. 'With my glass I recognise their many differences from the Nucutanis. It is amazing what they have done here. The task would have been enormous. The clearing is about a hundred metres wide and about a kilometre in length. It must have taken years to build. First they would have to clear the forest on each side of the river. Then they would have had to dig two huge channels, one each side of the river a hundred metres wide and a kilometre long. Next they diverted the river at the northern end into the two channels, and then diverted these back into one again at the southern end. Finally, piles of rocks have been placed at the centre at the far end to prevent the river following its original course, even when it floods. It would be very difficult and I think that many men would have died before it was completed. I can also see two bridges midway. These were built afterwards to carry the soil taken from the channels back into the centre, making an island with very fertile soil. Their village is now in the centre of that island and above the flood line. I can see crops being grown there. Now they have an island fortress guarded by the river each side. In it are fish for the taking. They have the surrounding forest for all their other needs and bridges to take them there. Those same bridges are guarded to keep out intruders. I can see the guards with my telescope. It is a marvellous feat of engineering, Martin. It was well thought out and has survived, however much nature would attempt to resume its original path. Even though I have heard evil stories about them I have to admire them.

'I also recognise differences in their appearances from the Nucutanis. I think we have solved the mystery of some of those photographs in our father's collection, Martin. They were taken of these people, but not on this island. That was built much later, after William Lockwood left.' José stared silently for a moment and then carried on. 'I wonder if the idea of all this was his idea when he stayed here. Did he make a drawing and the elders carried out the work after he left? There is no doubt that this is the village that he went to after his stay with the Nucutanis, but it was before the diversion.'

I could see that José was as amazed as I was at the ingenuity of it all and the part our father may have had to spur them on to carry out the work.

'They sound very clever and resourceful,' I said. 'Are they so evil, Jose?'

'Yes,' he replied. 'It has all been done at the expense of others. In the fields, I can see forest people from other tribes. They are chained to each other and there are men in charge with whips to punish them if they slack. I would say these are just a few of the people that have constructed this Garden of Eden for them. Many more must have died in the process. I would say this is one of the largest tribes in isolation. I think they have used some of their captives to inject new blood and increase their numbers. I can only imagine what happened to these new fathers once they had performed their duties to create new offspring. Their fate would not be as yours or our father's afterwards.' I started to get the picture even as he spoke. It was not so far-fetched as it sounded. The Nazis attempted to create an Arian race by selection. Animals such as lions go beyond their own pride to prevent inbreeding; I broke into my own thoughts.

'Can I look for myself with your telescope, Jose?'

He thought for a moment and then passed me his glass.

'Be very careful, Martin, I think they have lookouts on a tower in the centre of the village, keep one hand over the end to prevent the glass from giving our position away.'

He looked most concerned but felt he couldn't refuse my request; I had travelled this far and had endured the same hardships as himself.

Taking no chances, I took off my backpack and rifle and hid them in the undergrowth well away from where I intended going. I crawled on hands and knees to within a few yards of the opening. After removing my camera from a side pocket, I stood and moved forward to where José had stood and shielded the telescope as he had instructed. Everything he described was true, and the slave labour to build this Utopia was in evidence in the fields toiling in the hot sun with young guards patrolling amongst them, striking them with whips if they slacked. One body lay on the ground motionless. I raised my camera and clicked away. The distance was too far for detail but enlargements on my computer would disclose what was going on. I retreated carefully and put the camera and telescope into my backpack prior to joining José and safety. Stupidly I thought I'd risk one more look without the scope before I returned to José. My gaze took in the panoramic view of what had been an amazing undertaking. I knew no more. I was suddenly seized from behind and something heavy hit the side of my head. Just before I lost consciousness my nose detected that special smell of forest people. In that split second I knew these would not be as friendly as the Nucutanis.

Chapter 20

I heard the scream and then I opened my eyes. My head ached but all my limbs and faculties appeared intact. I was bound hand and foot in a sitting position and my boots and socks had been removed. I appeared be in the centre of the village that a few moments before I had looked at through José's telescope. I knew I wasn't a guest. Obviously time had passed since that moment and I was tethered to a post. I was now an uninvited guest of the Winukanatu tribe. Opposite me but tied to a wooden cross, his arms bound to the crossbeam and his ankles to the bottom of the post was José Barcelos. Blood oozed from wounds on his back and chest and his head sagged forward. He was unconscious and naked. The images of Jesus were called to mind.

The man who had beaten him was looming over me waiting for me to recover consciousness, whip in hand. It was this, applied to the soles of my feet that had woken me. It was I who had screamed. He leaned closer and his breath was foul. He muttered questions and pointed to the limp body of my brother. I couldn't understand him of course, and this seemed to annoy him more. He struck me once more with no emotion.

In the background, a small cluster of wizened elders seemed to be questioning his treatment but he scorned them. I didn't need to be an interpreter to understand the chain of command; dog's breath was in charge.

The elder's protestations were interspersed with the word Halok and this, no doubt, was the name of our tormentor. I adopted the same imploring attitude and called him by this name, nodding towards José for mercy. I got the impression, later confirmed, that he had taken over the tribe years ago, despite his youth. It was obvious all were afraid of him. I suspected he was the reason this tribe had become feared over the years. He put his head to one side at my attempt at his name. It was something I learned at Oxford during a business seminar. Try to get on first name terms with your competitor; it either annoys them or disarms them, but they do listen. For now I was happy to try anything to avoid punishment, grovelling would soon follow.

I heard a groan and José opened his eyes. He saw Halok, whip in hand, standing over me and shouted as best he could in Nucutani dialect and pointed to me. He carried on in this manner for some time and when he mentioned my surname it seemed to strike a chord in the budding Torquemado. José seemed to intimate that I was too good to be punished and that it was he, José, who deserved to be harmed for bringing me here. I could interpret as much by his actions and pointing. I started to get worried for him. He pointed to various parts of his own body. It appeared he wanted them to cut his throat and put his eyes out and even worse. At least the monster lowered his whip. He studied what José was saying and his heavy brow furrowed. I thought we were saved. Unfortunately,

José may have gone a bit too far, because Halok became agitated again, even smiling in a sadistic manner. Something in Jose's last remark made him snarl. He shouted an order. At his side were a small group of what was obviously his personal entourage. Young men that were willing to carry out his every whim. Young initiates that wished to emulate him. They seemed to be waiting to obey his every command. Four of them ran forward. Two of them undid the ropes fastening me to the post and I was dragged unceremoniously across the rough ground to a small hut away from the main arena and thrown in, still tied hand and foot.

I'd noticed this special unit of initiates were unlike some of the young men of the tribe. The latter were standing amongst the villagers behind the elders. They too had one lip pierced, similar to the ones in the Nucutani village after passing their initiation ceremony and were ready to become betrothed. It was quite clear that these elite warriors had been hand-picked by Halok. They were bigger than the rest and had two lip piercings, together with other disfigurements to their ears and noses. Moreover, they had a blue scar on their upper arms, some on the left and some on the right, perhaps denoting rank. I thought of the photo of my father in those later pictures with a similar mark, black on the photograph, and I froze. My mind was in turmoil. At that moment, José's shadow filled the opening and he was thrown in beside me, his wrists and ankles tied tightly. He was no longer naked, but wrapped in a rough blanket. There was a door on our prison, for that's what it was. It was firmly shut and we heard a pole being placed in position to prevent escape. This was a purpose-built prison of wooden saplings. It would be solitary confinement for whoever displeased Halok and the prospect of returning to Manaus seemed remote.

There were no windows and little else except loose straw covering the floor. It stank to high heaven and we discovered why shortly after. At the back, former inmates had used it as a toilet as there was no sanitation. Few attempts had been made to keep the place clean. There was a small shaft of light from a small hole one of its unfortunates had made at the back. It threw a theatrical spotlight onto the centre of the hut, about a foot across; otherwise the prison was devoid of sunlight. Despite this, insects found it suitable for their purpose. I longed immediately for the forest and my friends, the mosquitoes and piums. None of these creatures ventured near the spotlight for recognition. Most of them were enjoying feeding on the excrement at the back. A movement and a groan near the door told me José was still alive.

'Are you alright, Jose?' I said stupidly. His affirmative answer, weaker and through cracked lips, confirmed it. Crablike, I went over to him and placed myself back to back with him. I grasped his ropes and dragged him slowly and painfully towards the circle of light to inspect his wounds. Already, small creatures had smelled the stale blood under the blanket. Half lying, I adjusted my position so that his bound hands were against my belt buckle. There was no time to waste.

'Can you undo my buckle?' I asked. He didn't question my reason for the request but did as he was told. He shrugged off the blanket and set about the task. After many contortions, the belt became loose. I could tell the effort was aggravating his sore body. I had spent enough time with him to know of his resilience. I re-positioned myself till my zip was level with his hands.

'Now undo the top button and take hold of the zip.' Despite our plight, I smiled to myself at what may be going through his mind at that moment. I had no intention of telling him. Time was precious. The button was released and as soon as I knew he had gripped the tag of the zip, I drew myself away from him and the zip opened to the bottom. I moved back towards him until my thigh was touching him. I suppressed laughing out loud at this point, but by now he guessed what I was up to. He groped around till his fingers found the object of the exercise, my Swiss knife, what else?

It was something I had used very little during the journey but I had boasted about its many attributes to my brother. He knew it had been my father's and had accompanied him too. It was one of the reasons I'd been lured to the Amazon and Manaus. Perhaps now it would show its worth. He fumbled with the mechanism, looking for the blade. It was my turn to be apprehensive because of the knife's proximity to my vital external organs. He laughed a little through his cracked lips knowing this. I heard a click and it was he who manoeuvred so that he could place the blade between my wrists. The sharp blade made short work of the fibres, and apart from a small cut on my hand I was free. I rubbed the wrists quickly for a few seconds and set about releasing him from his bonds. The shared relief was almost tangible. I examined him as best I could and by now open sores from the lashing were attracting more of the insects. I tore off a large strip from my shirt.

'Can you piss?' I said. 'If so, piss into this.' Although parched he managed a trickle into the rag. I reinforced it with some of my own urine; after all we were brothers. He had no objection. Ignoring his pain, I scrubbed the red lines front and back. He bit his lip as the insects were dispersed. I peeled off my shirt and handed it to him. Without a word he put it on and buttoned up what was left of it. I felt reasonably satisfied that the danger of infection had at least been reduced.

'Well José, do you think we should make our escape now or wait till it gets dark?' He sat for a few moments thoughtfully, waiting for the sting of the crude treatment to his wounds to subside.

'You are indeed a true son of our parent William Lockwood. I was in despair when I was thrown in here. What I said to Halok would not have made him let us go. He wanted to kill us there and then. There was only one way to stop that happening. I used the knowledge I have learned about all these forest people including the Nucutanis. Death and sacrifices are usually the ends for animals; the larger the animal, the greater the glory. Children, women and then men are each greater in turn for sacrifices to the gods. Other tribe members are even better and white strangers are at the top of the list. He couldn't resist my plea for such an ending especially with the elders and the rest of the villagers listening. I knew it would only mean delaying our deaths but it was the only thing I could think of. If we don't escape, our end will be worse, burned alive perhaps. I am sorry, Martin, I couldn't explain to you at the time, it was the only thing I could think of to save our lives at that moment.

'Perhaps we can take advantage of this delay. Now that the Swiss knife has freed us, perhaps we can avoid our sacrifice too. I have more to tell you from the ranting of Halok and some of the others. But we must plan our escape quickly.'

At that moment we heard shouting in the distance and José held his finger up in a silent gesture. He listened carefully and whispered.

'The language is difficult for me but I think one of the guards is bringing us food. We must be kept healthy for the sacrifice. That I do know from the Nucutanis' ways. The gods would be angry otherwise. We will lie in the position we were left here as if tied, and hope he does not notice.'

We moved towards the back of the hut with me first facing the door. The smell of stale faeces was even stronger. If the guard came in to examine us I would see him in the spotlight. I grasped the knife by its familiar dimpled handle, determined to use it if necessary. I wondered if my dad had ever used it in anger. I think we both hoped the guard wouldn't venture into the stink of the prison and I wouldn't have to resort to using it.

The door opened and I knew my bravado attitude was a waste of time. The sunlight blinded me and I nearly added to the pile of excrement. The darkness returned and the theatre-like spotlight focussed on a large, black beetle that had entered when the door opened. We located the two objects left by our warder. One was a bowl of stew mixed in with a mash of cassava and the other a crude pottery jug containing a liquid. José smelled it and said it was a potent mixture that would make us feel happy enough to go to our sacrifice without a worry. It would be best not to drink it, he said. The food was OK, he added and proceeded to eat some of it. I joined him. With the knife I managed to cut a small hole at the front of the hut and could see that preparations were going ahead for the main event. Fires were already being lit and what looked like an altar had been dragged centre stage. I think it was being cleaned down from the last performance. I passed on the information to José, putting a funny slant on things because of my hysteria. I asked José to take a look. He peered through and watched the activity.

'Now that we have been fed, they will not disturb us until they drag us to the altar. They will all get drunk first and get into a party mood. We have about three to four hours before that. It will be a festive occasion for the whole village. We shall have to move pretty soon if we have to break out of our prison before that. It is already getting dark so that will help. First we must make a hole at the back of the hut towards the forest in case there are guards waiting for us.'

I had already started before he spoke. It wasn't a high security prison. Those sentenced accepted their punishment and the conditions were not too upsetting for them. Where could they go if they escaped? They had to cross a river in either direction and civilisation was not an option for them. It would be like trying to escape from Devil's Island. Forest life was all they knew and they would accept their punishment stoically.

The flimsiness of the walls bore this out; it was no more than woven saplings. The difficult part was working near the toilet. I insisted on doing most of the work and told José to keep a look out as a precaution. In half an hour, I had a hole big enough to crawl through. It was not quite dark.

I cut José's blanket into two parts. Making a hole in one I placed it over his head. He wrapped the rest around his waist as a skirt. I made holes in it and threaded the bindings that had been used to fasten our hands and feet as a belt. We waited

215

a further half an hour and crawled into the blackness. The darkness was a double-edged sword. It helped our escape but made progress difficult – we were in unknown territory and each step could spell danger. This time it was José who went first and I let him. He was more used to the rainforest than I. The immediate area was low vegetation on the outskirts of the village and only planted since the island was formed. Behind this was the forest proper with all its dangers. What lay under foot I hardly dared thinking about. I was glad José was leading.

We halted behind a variety of cedar. I recognised the pleasant mild pungency. They were planted like an orchard in rows and obviously were part of a pleasant retreat for the villagers. Everything had been thought out in this Shangri-La.

After the smell of the prison it was perfume. Neither of us had spoken since I'd set to work on the rear of the prison hut. It was José who broke the silence. It was noticeable that the positive manner and assurance that had given confidence to all his clients, and myself was less in evidence. He also spoke more quietly, but perhaps that was because of the situation and the result of his beating.

'You have done very well, Martin, and I have much admiration for you. Now we have to make sure that we are not recaptured. We will not be so lucky the next time.' Despite his beating he sounded resolute and his inbuilt survival instincts were beginning to surface. His years of experience in the forest were already beginning to pay off.

'I have a plan and want you to listen and see if you think it is the best idea. We are a team now and it's for your safety too. What you did for my wounds and how we escaped I shall never forget, even these clothes!' His laugh was not much more than a whisper, but his sense of humour had returned. I knew whatever he said would be sound and well thought out. I gave a murmur of approval. He was the professional once more and knew the forest and the ways of these people. I appreciated this extra trust that was now apparent, for what he was proposing. He asked me to visualise the scene as we had looked down on the village of the Winukanatu people.

'You remember the river and that it runs almost directly from north to south and has been split to encompass their village and then becomes one again. Eventually it joins the Rio Negro at Aldeia Vila Batista. We are now very near the bottom end of the eastern arm of this river that Halok and his people have formed. I think we must risk making our way south and across to the western arm. I saw boats along there. The whole village should be engaged in readiness for the night's festivities. If we arrive before they have noticed our escape, we could take one. It will be risky I know, but could be to our advantage if we want to outwit them. Once we have reached the river where it becomes one again, we can cross to the eastern bank. When they discover the boat is missing they will come after us down the western side of the main river towards Aldeia Vila Batista, for this is the main town for tourists. They will guess this is where we are heading for, the safety of that town. If I am right, we can abandon the boat, then take to the forest in a westward direction. We will release the boat downstream and with luck it will continue towards Aldeia Vila Batista. If they do catch it up, that is where they will think we have gone. Meanwhile we will circle back on foot through the forest towards where we were captured. They will not expect us to do that. We need those backpacks if we are to survive the return journey. That is why we should risk stealing a boat from the west side; it should fool them. Once we have found our backpacks we can return the way we came, through the forest. All we have to do then is to follow the trail we have marked until we reach the boat. We should not have to worry about pursuers. What do you think Martin?' I gripped his arm in the dark.

'It sounds good to me,' I whispered, 'let's do it.'

Chapter 21

We have rarely travelled through the forest before during the night. For most of the predators it was their finest hour. The air would be full of bats, moths as big as birds, and other airborne creatures were a danger. At ground level there was every sort of crawling insect including leeches, and snakes of course. Even José never ventured out during the hours of darkness, he said. But there was no option. We couldn't wait till daylight. Whatever fate awaited us in the darkness it had to be better than the one arranged by Halok and his merry men.

José led the way armed with a sturdy truncheon-like branch with a natural bulbous end, quickly fashioned with my knife. I had this same knife at the ready for man or beast. My thoughts were Rambo but my actions were unlikely to emulate him. Unfortunately my gun was in my backpack. I would have felt more courageous with that.

We moved from east to west, keeping the lights of the village in sight through the copse of cedars. The smell was pleasant and I felt less threatened by what could be underfoot. José was in the crude outfit I had fashioned for him and neither of us had footwear. It would have felt suicidal under any other circumstances. I concentrated on the shadowy figure in front with frequent glances to the fires of the village, hoping to shut out the forest dangers. It was a cloudy night and almost a full moon. It flashed on and off like a lighthouse beacon continuously between each cloud, making progress hazardous. We would freeze in unison each time it illuminated the scene. It had its advantages of course. The moonlight lit up the village and from our vantage point we had a panoramic view of enemies should there be any; man or beast. Eventually I spotted two boats moored at the southern end of the western channel. There were others at intervals further up and no doubt others dotted around the island for transportation to and from the man-made island. There was about fifty yards of open ground with only low crops between our cover in the cedars and the boats. José stopped and I drew level with his shoulder. We waited for a reasonable interval of moonlight to survey the scene in detail and to memorise it. He touched my shoulder and indicated the boats that were our ultimate objective. I nodded to show that I'd understood what he had in mind. The whites of his eyes seem to glow in the dark. I felt sure they could be seen from the village. Such was my fear.

We stopped for a few minutes and watched for any sign of activity between our target and us, or any there. The noise from the cluster of huts was now quite audible. It was probable that everyone in the village would want to watch the sacrifice and this was to the good.

There was more than one fire and the sky was lit up. Halok and his handpicked entourage would be anticipating the bloodletting and the orgy that would follow the human sacrifice later. Like a Roman emperor, it would raise his stature in their eyes.

When the Winukanatus had bifurcated the river, they had the sense to build up the island they had created with the soil removed. This levee prevented flooding, a continuous threat in the rainforests. We had both admired them for that and it was another added benefit for us at that moment.

We climbed down the embankment and silently thanked them for their foresight. We could keep to the water's edge and not be seen as we approached the boats. José was leading and I close behind. As we came within sight of the first boat, the moon came out once again and more of the ingenuity of these people became apparent. A launching ramp had been cut from the top of the levee to the water level. Cross poles had been sunk in and boats could be hauled up the ramp for repairs, or to avoid floodwaters that were always waiting to cause destruction. There would be others of these ramps of course. We were ten yards from our objective and looking upwards for the moon to disappear. A large cloud started to edge across it and it was our opportunity. The ramp was clear and crouching down, we crept towards the first boat. There are various boats used by Amerindians throughout the whole of South America. The most common is the small one painstakingly cut from a log. This was one of the larger ones, more like a canoe. I had seen one in the village of the Nucutanis. These are made from laths of wood covered with skins and sealed with a rubber solution. They are fairly light and can be carried easily by two men. Sometimes outriggers made of bamboo are added for stability. The Nucutanis were far from water but had such boats. On occasion they would go on fishing trips. This was such a boat.

I was glad José was in front. As he went to step into the boat a figure stood up and stretched his arms out, yawning. It was quite unexpected. We hadn't seen any sign of life and had thought that everyone would be at the party. He could have been a guard to prevent intruders and Halok wasn't the sort to let security lapse. He must have been dozing on duty in the bottom of the boat and stood to keep awake, otherwise he would have had the advantage over us. As it was I was rooted to the spot. It was José who reacted first and struck high up with his crude truncheon. The man fell sideways, but quickly recovered. As he rose with a roar, José struck him again. Still not out of the fight, he grabbed Jose's foot as he lay there. José fell backwards, hitting his head on the side of the boat. The villager was quickly on top. It all happened in a few seconds. I watched it in slow motion, rooted to the spot. I was watching a film, engrossed and inactive, yet suddenly, without thinking it seemed afterwards, I moved forward and brought my knife down into the man's back. He twisted round as if to squash a hornet that had stung him. I felt helpless. *He was a monster, without feeling.* Below him, José grabbed the rings in his adversary's lips. His scream was muffled as José twisted the rings. I plunged my knife into the side of his neck once more. This time blood spurted out and even though I couldn't see it I felt the warm liquid hit my face as it squirted between my clenched fist and his neck. I could taste it and I felt sick. The man shuddered and lay prone across José, who heaved him off and over the side where the outrigger had caught him. My face was covered in blood, and the smell was vile; I threw up. José tore off his skirt and wiped the gore off my face. He leaned over the edge of the boat, wet the cloth and wiped some more. He dropped the bloodstained skirt and hugged me. Even he was trembling.

Half an hour later we were gliding gently with the current, away from the Winukanatu village. Trailing in our wake was a second bloodstained canoe with the body of the dead guard in it. Despite a lump on the side of his head, José recovered quickly and was even cheerful regarding our prospects. He had discarded the bloodstained skirt and it was in the canoe behind us with the dead guard. We'd left no evidence of the incident and with luck perhaps we wouldn't be connected to the disappearance of the boats. We hoped that initially, Halok would send our pursuers into the forest behind the empty prison cell. I fashioned fresh clothes for José from blankets found on the two canoes. He was steering at the back. I sat in the centre covered in a blanket for warmth. I had shivered uncontrollably after the death of the guard, and was still shaking every few minutes. José was talking all the time to raise my spirits. So much had happened since my trauma. He had fully recovered.

He'd assessed the situation as if the dead man was not a problem. While still naked, he had hauled the corpse into the bottom of the canoe. He took the knife from my still clenched fist and washed it in the water as if it had been used for a meal. He released the second canoe and brought it alongside. I was transfixed, looking at the dead body. He told me to get into the fresh one. I did so. He paddled it forward and tied the bloodstained one behind.

'There was only one guard,' he said matter-of-factly. 'Now we'll get rid of all signs of him and us.' As I watched he retraced his steps to where we'd emerged from the undergrowth. I watched him as he tore a large fern from the ground and removed all traces of our footprints till he reached the canoes. He carried out all this work dressed only in the shawl I had fashioned for him in the prison, over his head and around his shoulders. As the moon emerged from behind the clouds I glimpsed his naked silhouette from the rear carrying out these movements. In retrospect it was hilarious and I would tell him about it much later. At that moment I was wondering if I would ever recover from murdering another human being.

The current was in our favour, flowing as it did from north to south in a fairly leisurely fashion till it reached the Rio Negro. The channel we were on after our escape very soon joined its other half. José released the other canoe after discharging its cargo. Little would be left of it in a few days, he said. This is certainly the place to get rid of a body. He slashed holes in the sides of the boat and hoped it would slowly sink or be found floundering by their pursuers, more false evidence of our demise. Otherwise the boat would stay on course till it reached Aldeia Vila Batista. If Halok followed, it was hoped he would give up before that, thinking we had made good our escape. Or if he caught up with the boat, maybe drowned. He certainly wouldn't enter the town. It was all supposition of course, but it was clutching at the straws of hope.

After seeing the other canoe safely on its way, José steered our canoe to the east bank. We hauled the boat ashore and deep into the forest for over an hour. We concealed it as best we could and he said we should rest up till it became light. I was still in a daze and said little. He searched in the vicinity and found fruit and an empty gourd that he filled with rainwater. I sipped a little of the water and wondered if I would ever get my appetite back. My stomach felt full thinking about that blood and that muffled moan from the man I stabbed. José had found a suitable tree with many branches and we contrived a makeshift bed about six feet up. It was the best we could do and I didn't care if I was attacked in the night at that moment. José covered me with a blanket and lay down beside me. He laid his arm across my chest and murmured a few bars of a song that was obviously something he had heard as a child by his mother. I remembered my own mother singing me to sleep on a few occasions. I thought about those times, and then my dad, and I felt real bad. I cried, gently at first and then sobbed. José kept on singing quietly and I went to sleep. I cried with the horror of my crime. I cried with shame for the man I had killed. I asked for forgiveness.

Chapter 22

The whole episode unfolded before me when I awoke. But this wasn't university and there was no one to remind me of last night's weaknesses. José had been up for some time. He had modified his attire with my knife and some skilful use of strands from a soft bark. He had also made two pairs of woven sandals from raffia. He was wearing one pair and mine were tied on before we set off. Despite his part in the affair he seemed to have recovered. His apparent normality rubbed off on me and I started to rationalise about last night's episode. This was not Cornwall or Yorkshire or any other part of Britain. There would be no hue and cry by the police. Halok and his village would not report us. They would make every effort to track us down and wreak revenge in their own way. There were no witnesses and the unfortunate guard's body would quickly disappear. Life was cheap out here. I knew I had to concentrate in the job on hand. José was the only witness and we were partners in the crime. We had no fear of being found out by the loose tongue of an associate. That was usually the downfall of criminals.

We had to find our way to the same spot before our capture and subsequently back to Manaus. That was our biggest problem. In the light of a new day and with Jose's efforts before I was awake, it was all that was necessary to bring me back from my black thoughts.

'We cannot light a fire,' he said. 'It is best if we go now and eat as we progress. The further we get away from here the better. We may have underestimated Halok. A dictator he may be, but what he has done for his people shows he is resourceful and cunning. He may be already coming this way. Our escape will not be good for his ego. The villagers will be showing him their disappointment.' I saw his point. They have been denied a rare spectacle. 'They will expect him to recapture us and be sacrificed,' he finished.

'It will be like a Roman Emperor having no gladiators in the Coliseum.' I said. He laughed too loud for safety, given our circumstances.

'You have not lost your Oxford wit,' he said. He moved off without waiting for a response and I followed. Yesterday never happened. He called on his forest craft, both ancient and modern, to get his bearings. He had no compass or maps of any description. He was relying on instinct. Once more, time was of no consequence to our progress. We weren't in a desert with no food or water. Our only enemy was the vastness of the forest and those adversaries after our flesh. Nevertheless, the wherewithal for survival was all around us. At times on that first day I sensed we were sometimes going around in circles, but what do I know? All trees look alike and there were no signposts. José's brow was furrowed from time to time, but if he was lost he never conveyed his thoughts to me. He knew I was in low spirits and smiled from time to time.

We said very little, he because of his effort to find the spot from where we were abducted without running into a scout from the Winukanatu village. We were constantly on the alert, standing like statues at the slightest crack of a twig or movement in the canopy of the trees.

We could have saved ourselves this added danger simply by locating José's boat and returning to Manaus, thankful that it was all over. José knew my backpack was important and he hoped his own hadn't been spotted when we were captured. Their contents would be very useful on our return journey. To reach them would be a triumph over Halok. To leave my camera would have been a disaster for me personally, and the equipment was essential if we wanted to make the return easier. All we had now was what we stood up in, normally inadequate in the rainforest. José and I had to rely on our personal efforts.

There are always surprises in the vast rainforest. We came to one of those clearings that were unexpected even to José because of its size. It was two hundred metres across and roughly circular. A huge standing of trees had been cleared. From the debris left behind, they had been walnut trees, illegally felled. By the state of the rotting branches, this had occurred at least ten years ago. Since then, José said someone else had excavated the ground and left a huge crater that was now filled with water.

'I think at the time of the tree felling, some company official visited the site and thought he detected signs of a mineral below ground. Multi-nationals are always on the lookout for such opportunities. Further excavations were carried out and it came to nothing. From the plants surrounding the pool this area has been flooded in the past. I think I see signs of activity in the pool.'

On closer inspection we saw small fish and shrimps. It was a cloudless day and I was pleased when he suggested we have a decent rest away from the humid atmosphere of the forest. He said we were roughly midway between where we had abandoned the two canoes and where we were taken prisoner. By his attitude I think he was now on track. It was unlikely our pursuers would be anywhere near this area. We still had a huge task and how we'd suffered as captives was beginning to tell. Once more it was a matter of dogged determination and seeing out the hand we'd been dealt. Our minds were at one with that. We felt recuperation was in order.

There seemed little danger from the inhabitants of the pool and we waded in, it was no more than two feet deep. The idea came to us both at the same time and soon we had skilfully caught an array of titbits for a snack. With trepidation I had to follow José's method for eating them as he was still avoiding lighting a fire. It was an added precaution and worth sticking to at the moment.

'When we have all our equipment, including the machetes and your rifle, we will be more prepared to meet them. Now we are at a disadvantage.'

Jose took the catch of fish and simply cut off the heads and tails with the knife. He slit them from end to end, emptied out the innards and chewed away, finally spitting out the bones. Two or three of the shrimps were enough for me; sushi has never been high on my fish menus. I finished off with fruit.

José seemed to enjoy the bounty and ate his fill, laughing at the face I pulled before I gave up. We made a temporary bed in the fork of a convenient tree, as was usual in these circumstances, adding a rope ladder from lianas for added safety; the bed was six feet off the ground. We settled in for the night early and hoped we would feel fresher for it in the morning. It was only when I was dozing off when a thought struck me. Why weren't there any animals or birds around the water hole? Surely what we had eaten would be food for them. I found out early next morning. There is not much satisfaction in hindsight.

Chapter 23

My stomach was in knots and I knew it was diarrhoea, I also felt sick. It was the same symptoms I had after my first night with the Nucutanis. Dawn had scarcely broken and I climbed over the side towards where I knew the crude ladder was. I descended as quickly as possible hoping to reach ground before my bowels exploded. I almost fell over José, who had preceded me. He was laying full length on the mosses a few yards from the bottom of the tree where we'd spent our night. He too was a victim of the same problem as myself. He'd managed to throw off his skirt but too late to squat. He was moaning and in a bad way, worse than me, that I could tell. I had to get rid at both ends before I could attend to him, and when I did I could see he was past moaning and had almost passed out. José was made of sterner stuff than me and he needed help. There were no Nucutani womenfolk to administer their wonder drugs. All I could hope for was that José knew what to do in the circumstances. He was barely conscious when I returned to him. I hauled him back towards the tree and sat him up against it. It was one of those trees with a basal swelling covered with lichen and mosses and not too uncomfortable.

Gone was his golden tan, to be replaced with a grey pallor. His eyes rolled in their sockets and he didn't know I existed. I asked him if there was anything available that might help his condition. He gabbled out words and I had to lean forward to understand what they meant. He focussed his eyes on me and pointed to a silver birch-like sapling in the half-light and I realised he had been crawling towards it when he collapsed. The trunk was covered in a black fungus and it was this he'd been after. I understood, and tore off a handful of the slimy growths and brought them back. When he nodded I fed one into his mouth. With difficulty he managed to swallow a couple of mouthfuls. He nodded again as if to indicate it was enough. I then became aware of my own plight. I sprayed the undergrowth once more but I knew my plight was mild compared to José's. It was the fish that had upset us and he'd consumed considerably more than me. I climbed the ladder and fetched a blanket down. With the ever-faithful knife I cut a square and soaked it with rainwater that conveniently gathers in some of the large leaves. I cut off one of them and carried it back to José. He sipped from it and I bathed the stench from his body. He had already felt the benefit of his medicine and the retching was subsiding. I knew he needed no further medication or he would have told me.

By now the sun had appeared over the horizon and we sat side-by-side recovering slowly. As my symptoms receded I replenished the water and after several journeys I had made us both look and feel more respectable.

An hour later he was fit to talk and his brain had already been busy. He blamed himself for not noticing the absence of animals at the pool and asked if I was OK. The black fungus was only a very strong emetic and would get rid of all the poisons that had caused the upset. He asked me to search for plants that would have a soothing and nutritious effect. These would be what the village women had dosed me with. He described them to me and after a few trips back and forth he was satisfied he had the necessary ingredients. He mixed various ones, and mashed them together on a stump to make the concoction. We both swallowed a portion of the mixture and rested in the sunshine of the clearing, away from the stench. Now and then I fetched fresh water and in a remarkably short time, we felt fit enough to wash our clothes and ourselves. We sat for another couple of hours while our laundry dried out. Our only activity was swatting at a few persistent insects with fronds of ferns. Most of their friends were enjoying the mess we'd left at the bottom of the tree. When we returned, most of it had disappeared, courtesy of some dung beetle. In the forest, one creature's waste is another one's meal. We collected a few cassava roots and after peeling and cleaning, we chewed them and spit out the pulp. The carbohydrates would sustain our energy till the next day when we should be back to reasonable fitness. We climbed back to our sleeping quarters and hauled up the ladder after us. It was still early so we talked about tomorrow and hoped there would be no more disasters like today. We took it in turns to sleep. We certainly wouldn't be doing any marching today.

I felt pretty lousy when the dawn chorus of howlers and other canopy dwellers woke us the next morning. My stomach was raw and I'm sure my breath smelled like a cesspit, if José's was anything to go by. He looked worse than I felt. On top of that, he was worried and admitted it. It was the first time since

I'd met him back in Manaus that he'd lost a little of his self-assurance.

'The forest is very big, Martin, and I have not travelled it all. After our escape, if we had stayed on the river we would have come to Aldeia Vila Batista and the Rio Negro. I'm sure you could have found the river with no difficulty going with the current to Manaus. But because we crossed the river and made our way on foot through the forest it has me confused. I have no map and no compass. And until we recover them I am finding it difficult. We are not going in circles, but with only the sun to guide us until we find our tree markings, it is guesswork. It would be good if we could find a clue in this clearing to give me an idea roughly where we are. The men who worked here must have travelled from some town. They would have vehicles to carry tools and supplies and maybe returned each night into lodgings. If I knew in which direction they came from it would help. I do not want to waste our time walking around using energy up. We are still weak from this poison.' He looked to me for advice.

'Then why don't we spend the rest of the day having a good look round this site?' I suggested. 'I'll start from one end and you start from the other. Anything we find that is not part of the forest we'll pile up in the middle of the clearing. We'll do that for two hours unless something obvious appears. Then we'll have a little something to eat and start again.'

José smiled weakly. He seemed pleased that I was not dispirited after the poisoning episode and had confidence in him despite all our troubles. He smiled again at my philosophical attitude and how we might solve the problem. He was probably still blaming himself for his stupidity. My attitude assured him that I still had faith in him and that we would be OK. My suggestion sounded good sense, he agreed.

'I have already seen discarded rubbish these people have left and the animals can't have eaten everything they left behind. As you say, maybe we can find a clue. We won't starve or die of thirst, and there is not much point punishing ourselves further by going on.'

I felt like crap and he'd had more of the poison than me. Without another word we retreated towards the far corners of the clearing and set about our task. Good fortune finally smiled on us.

I had spent an hour searching the site from side to side and poking around in the soil. I'd found several empty packages and office memos that had been carelessly discarded. I carried them into the centre of the clearing for further investigations later and saw that José had done the same. Then I struck lucky. An empty oil drum caught my eye under a tree. It had been rolled there and was almost unnoticed in the undergrowth. It had a faded label still attached. On it was the address of the supplier. It was a company in the town of São António de Abunari. I ran over and told José. He followed me to my discovery and after investigating further we discovered a path, now overgrown, that had been used by vehicles. José's face lit up.

'I know this town. If I am right, we are midway between it and Aldeia Vila Batista; São António de Abunari is further north and to the east. Everything seems to fit, Martin.' His eagerness and the truth in this statement were contagious. We danced around the oil drum as if it was a Maypole. After our dance, he outlined what he had in mind.

235

'If we strike out north-west of this track we should be heading towards the reservation and eventually pick up our previous trail.'

I was confident of his assessment and we revelled in this new knowledge gained from the oil drum. Furthermore, neither of us felt the desire to dash off. Despite yesterday's disaster, we decided the clearing was an ideal spot for another night's stay. It was me who spoke next.

'Let's stay here for tonight, José, find a little food; fruit sounds good to me José. I'm sure my breath would kill a small animal at ten yards and yours is no better if you don't mind me telling you.'

He laughed to see that I was making light of the situation and he wasn't under pressure any more. We spent an hour in the immediate area of the forest and he excelled. We returned to the clearing with an array of delicious fruit and nuts.

With our dog's breath in mind he found a variety of lime, and I'm sure it did the trick. We ate the food and both of us felt more in the mood for tackling what lay ahead. After a rest, we found fresh water and generally cleaned ourselves up. Then a new bedroom, far away from the old and, despite having no home comforts or nightcap, we settled in for the night. I'm sure we felt better with our newfound knowledge.

Chapter 24

José never wavered from his previous day's judgment as to which direction to take as we stood in that clearing. Nevertheless it was a week before we finally saw one of our tree markings. It was remarkable really and despite his years of trekking through the forests, José jumped for joy like some schoolboy; I joined in. We'd had some rough days. Our clothes were practically falling apart with sweat and mildew. There was plenty of water but not in sufficient quantities to have a good wash. We squelched through boggy forest terrain in raffia footwear that needed constant repair. We strapped pieces of bark to them to prevent thorns from piercing them. Our only tool or weapon was the beautiful Swiss knife and I thanked my father for it every day. José called it God whenever we made use of it.

One day I screamed out, thinking it was a large thorn. When we looked, it was a sting from something. The pain persisted and it swelled up. José made up a poultice and it took away the pain but it took a day and a half before I could walk without hobbling. I woke each morning wondering if I would ever reach civilisation again without an amputation, or worse.

One day we hardly made any progress at all because of torrential rain that obscured the sun.

We trudged along without even speaking to save energy. José would hold up his hand to call a halt, leaving me to rest while he studied the sun or the lichen on the trees to get a bearing. He would walk on his own to the left or to the right through the trees for inspiration, leaving me to mark the spot where we'd halted. It would be twenty minutes or so before he returned. I would hear his special howler monkey impersonation and reply till he located me. We still weren't taking any chances of being discovered by people, hostile or friendly.

Mostly we followed worn trails made by animals but sometimes we had to cut a path through lianas that barred our path. God in the form of the Swiss knife came to our rescue. At that moment, if someone had asked me what day it was I couldn't have said. I was fairly despondent but hadn't lost faith in my half-brother.

We both saw a perimeter trail marker together but it was José who remembered exactly in which direction was the next one. He could decipher which particular tree it was and which way the X was pointing. Then he became really excited. Soon, he said, we would arrive at one of our overnight camp sites. He described it in detail and I began to remember. It spurred us on. Despite it being another mile, we pushed on fast till we reached it. As we approached, it was like coming home.

The canopy opened up and there it was. A small stream ran through it from higher ground, forming a pool and then continuing on to join a larger one, and so on till it finally joined a river. José guessed it was fed from a spring higher up. As we approached, the animals using it left; slowly it seemed, almost as if they resented our intrusion. It was likely we were the only human beings they had ever seen, and here we were again to disturb their oasis. Even now they didn't feel threatened, and slowly wandered off into the forest as we made our appearance. I wished I had my gun if only to show them who was boss. We stayed two days and completely recovered.

José set traps in the trees around and the following morning after breakfast came back with a squirrel. Lunchtime was a feast. He demonstrated his skill at starting a fire without his supply of lighters. I'd seen various versions of natives in New Zealand and other countries on TV but was a little sceptical. With his instructions, I fashioned a nine-inch long stick with a point at each end for the spindle. This would be rotated at a fast rate by a bow that looped around it. The bottom point of the spindle was held in a hollow of a fallen log. José pressed down on the top of it and I sawed away at a fast rate with the bow. He had crumbled some dry lichen around the bottom of the spindle and blew on it gently as it got hot. I was amazed as the white lichen turned brown and then smoked. Finally a small flame appeared and José added more fuel. We had our fire and I made sure it was stoked up. The canopy surrounding us was quite tall and José said it was doubtful if the smoke would rise above the trees. In any case we were still some distance from our objective, the village of the Winukanatus. As each day had passed since leaving their hostile environment, we felt less threatened. Halok would have thought of something to take the villager's mind off their disappointment and the event would be in their folklore by now. It was woe betide the next stranger who strayed into their path.

It was late afternoon before we ate the meal. It was a banquet. Roast squirrel in herbs. Except for the cassava, I had never seen the vegetables before. Afterwards fruit, including figs. All this was washed down with a fruit drink. During the afternoon after a suitable siesta we had a good wash and repaired our clothing where we could. José made some new rope soles from toughened liana creeper for our flimsy footwear and when we went to bed I felt less anxious than the previous week.

Things went better the next two days, but when José mentioned that we were getting close to our destination, my stomach churned. He looked forward to hopefully being re-united with his maps, compass and other essential equipment. To me it was a double-edged sword. If the camera was still intact I would be ecstatic, but in the back of my mind was the menacing figure of Halok and his elite personal bodyguards; they could be lying in wait. He didn't look the sort to be on the losing side and our escape wouldn't do anything for his prestige. His tribe would be looking forward to a couple of sacrifices. He had let them down. Maybe José too worried, but didn't show it. He was made of sterner stuff than me.

His concern was apparent however, on our approach to the village and he impressed on me the need to be silent. We made use of every scrap of cover. We crept low to the ground and José was meticulous as he placed each foot down. I was at his shoulder as usual and he pointed out twigs to avoid. Eventually, after a nerve-wracking hour, I saw the gap that denoted the clearing containing the raised village of the Winukanatus, surrounded by the divided river.

I expected us to continue and find our two backpacks. Instead, José's eyes swivelled from side to side slowly. Pointing to my eyes with his two fingers he encouraged me to do the same. We did this for a full ten minutes until suddenly we both detected a movement at the same time. Near the opening was one of Halok's elite with the unmistakeable blue mark on his arm. Blending in with his surroundings it was only because of his outstretched legs that we had spotted him. His *sentry box* was a slender pine, sheltered from the elements for the purpose. There would be several around the perimeter of the village. Perhaps this one had been set up for our return. It was twenty yards from the bushes containing our two backpacks, and hopefully they hadn't been detected. If they had, our arduous journey had been in vain. Even so, it would be impossible to retrieve them without him spotting us. José signalled for me to retreat away from the danger area. We did this equally as carefully as on our approach. When we were well out of range of the sentry we sat down on a fallen branch, completely out of sight.

'So there is someone waiting for our return, José?' I asked, apprehensively.

'No, I don't think so. Halok will have pursued us down river and think we have made good our escape. He will have thought up some entertainment to replace our escape and keep the villagers happy. It's the sort of thing the Nucutani elders did to avoid disappointments for their people. I could see our equipment is still where we left it. It would have been gone if they had seen it. We are very lucky, Martin. These guards will be permanent all around the village for intruders. I should have been aware of them when we first arrived here. That is why we were caught. Remember there was also one in the boat that almost took us unawares?' *How could I ever forget?* 'There is no way we can get our equipment, Martin, in the daylight. We must get completely out of range for the rest of the day. We will have some food and then when it is dark I will go back.'

I felt inadequate not being able to volunteer for the job, but I wasn't up to it; I knew that and José did too. It would have only been paying lip service so I didn't offer, and for two of us to go meant double the risk. He wouldn't have let me anyway.

I was on edge all day, but except for keeping our voices down to a whisper, José tried to act normally for my benefit. Nevertheless it was a long afternoon. Before he left we made provisions for sleeping quarters up a suitable tree. This was over two hundred yards from the sentry. He told me to stay up there and not to come down till he was beneath me and I was sure it was him. He said it lightly but I knew that he had considered being seen and not returning. When he asked if he could borrow my knife I realised how dangerous it was for him. I didn't argue and handed it over. As he disappeared with the knife in one hand and his cudgel in the other, I wondered if I would see him again. What I would do if he didn't return was my only selfish thought at that moment. How could I possibly find my way back to Manaus without him? At that moment it was the least of my worries.

The forest is never without noises and my muscles ached after a while, so intent was I to keep silent. Creatures moved above and below and I tried to keep track of time by counting my heartbeats. The rough and ready shelter of woven leaves did little to stop the rain from dripping onto me. I thought about home, girls I'd dated, university. Under my closed eyelids, I stood in front of my dad's marble gravestone. I had flipped though the photographs and in an almost spur-of-the-moment attitude decided to make this journey, as if I was going on holiday. Cowering up this tree, I realised how tough it had really been, and how lucky I was to have had José as my guide and protector. My brain raced through all my life, in a minute or so. There were no books to read, no television or radio, and time dragged.

The branches vibrated from above. I waved my arms to deter any creature that could be on their way down towards me. I couldn't shout even if my dry throat would have allowed me to because it would reverberate through the forest and reach the village, or so I reasoned. There were rustlings below. Was it a nocturnal creature searching for food or one of Halok's men? Had they killed José and were looking for me? Terror lost out to brain exhaustion and I must have dozed off. I dreamt I was on holiday with my mother in Wales. It was a rare occasion and we were about to take a journey in a steam train. The driver pulled on the cord and a whistle tooted. Then as he let off the brake, a cloud of steam enveloped the carriage with a hiss. I woke sweating with heat and fear. The hiss was below me. It was a snake. I grabbed a stick from beside me and raised it. In the gloom I made out the shadowy figure of José. He passed first one and then the other of the backpacks to me as he reached my side. He hugged me like a brother. I hugged him like a child after a bad dream. I asked him how he had managed to get them. He said he would tell me the following day. Perhaps he didn't want me to get nightmares.

Chapter 25

The next day saw us once more following the trail markers, each step leaving behind the terror of our encounter with Halok and the Winukanatus.

'I think I can find my way back to Manaus,' I said to José, almost hysterical with relief. His laugh was as loud as I remembered it from earlier in our journey. The contents of the backpacks were intact, and a shirt and pair of underpants replaced our temporary attire. It certainly helped to improve our appearance and morale. We looked forward eagerly to those oases that we had enjoyed on the outward journey and the first of these became a two-day break. It was one with a spring-fed pool in a small clearing. The sun came out as we entered. José said it was a coincidence, I wasn't so sure.

'I think the steamy forest precipitates the rain as it passes overhead. When the clouds reach a dry clearing, they pass over because of the dry air underneath.' He laughed out loud at the suggestion, but couldn't argue with my logic. And it had been true so far.

With the waterproofs from the packs we set up a camp in the clearing. We went together for fruits of the forest and I took the gun. With his knowledge and my accuracy we returned with food for another banquet. There was no hurry with the preparation. We stripped off and washed, then we rinsed our new clothes, already sweaty from our exertions. We left them to dry on a pile of branches in the centre of the clearing. Meanwhile, I built a fire and lit it with one of José's lighters; no rubbing two boy scouts together this time! By the time José had prepared the agouti for cooking, the smoke had disappeared and red-hot embers glowed. We skewered the carcase through the middle and spit-roasted it on the fire. This only took a few minutes and, with careful manoeuvring, I managed to cook it before setting fire to the skewer and having to renew it.

As we were naked, we ate food with our hands, with the juices flowing freely and laughing at such a sight. With his usual ingenuity, José came up with a special dry leaf he had found and rolled it into a cigar. I tried a couple of puffs but gave up. In the afternoon we got dressed with the newly laundered clothes. I couldn't believe that a short time ago they had been new. We enjoyed a second day there and felt ready to tackle anything when we set off again. The rains held off for a couple of days and I had more opportunities to take photographs of species I hadn't seen before. We were very near the line of the equator and at midday the heat was unbearable. Under the canopy of trees the humidity was total and breathing was difficult. If we found a gap caused by many of the natural fires, the temperature must have been well over forty degrees.

There are a thousand tributaries that feed the Amazon on its way to the sea. On a map they are veins that look insignificant. We encounter them all the time, some are large with the floodwater and some are almost dried up. I'm sure no map could be accurate at any one time. The one made use of by the Winukanatu tribe is such a tributary, wide though it is. The landscape is never boring. During that last day before we found the boat, still intact, I saw yet more coloured carpets of butterflies on the riverbanks. As they rise in the air when disturbed they undulate like a real carpet. They move to new pastures and settle again; it's a rare and beautiful sight.

José was like a small boy at Christmas opening his presents as we unwrapped his precious boat. Insects of all description had found their way in. Woodlice couldn't believe their luck till we squashed them. A mouse had made a nest and already had a litter of six pink blobs. It deserted them when we disturbed the nest. I placed the orphans in a tree bottom. They wouldn't survive ten minutes, but I hadn't the heart to destroy them. There were items of clothing José and I could improve our appearance with and all the equipment was in good order.

We hauled the boat through the forest that had become flooded again since we were last here, and for the most part it floated on its own. Before we had set off, he had studied the maps, his compass and the sun, which was high enough to point us in the right direction. Everything was so familiar that it could have been the high street. José looked assured now that he was captain of his ship again. He steered it to where he judged the nearest waterway was, that would lead us south and eventually to Manaus. I too felt very happy now. I even kidded myself that the land was becoming familiar and told him so. He laughed long and loud.

Except for subsidence and other natural soil erosion caused by the heavy rains, the Amazon and the countless waters that feed it are gentle to navigate. On this particular occasion, the boat meandered along at no more than two knots per hour in nautical terms. No power is needed now that we are going downhill, as I called it. José laughed again when I said this. We are away from the forest, and its myriad of soul-destroying insects. It's pleasant. I sit in the shadow of the canvas canopy and it could be June on a Thames river cruise. There is still a difference, of course. I can hear the howlers on the far shore cheering me on as if I'm coxing an Oxford crew. I never have, of course. The traumas are receding and I feel happier than I have done for some time. A turtle passes the boat; that's how slow we are going. I look up and José is smiling as if he can guess my pleasant thoughts.

'And who are you in bed with at the moment, Martin?'

I tell him how wrong he is and how different today is from some of our previous ones. I make an observation about the water that is gently shepherding us home.

'I was thinking, José; half of this water is probably first drawn up from the salty Pacific. The rest is from the tributaries as far away as Peru and many other countries in South America. It comes together and continues on till it reaches the Atlantic as fresh water. And so it has done for millions of years. Give or take a gallon or two, it's the same water recycled.' He nods but I'm not sure he agrees with me and perhaps I've simplified the process too much.

'And did your Oxford professor tell you why?' There was an answer to that, of course, but it was much too convoluted to begin to explain. I shook my head. We stopped in the afternoon for something to eat. How different it was now that we had the boat and all our equipment. I couldn't wait to show my skills at fishing as we moored in a tributary. I showed him my catch and asked which one he fancied. He picked out the one we were to eat and threw the rest back.

'I'll bet you wouldn't do that in the Thames,' he said. I lit a fire and in no time we were enjoying the fish, together with boiled and mashed cassava. Afterwards we threw the scraps overboard and its relatives thanked us very much and quickly consumed them. We finished off with fruit. All free of charge and not even a tip for the waiter. We sat for a while and José lit up. It was the first cigar he'd had since re-joining his beloved boat, and after the first lungful of smoke he gave a great sigh of pleasure. When he had finished the cigar he said he thought it would be a good idea if we called at a town called Repartimento. He thought our pursuers had given up by now. I could see that like me, the trauma and the stress of what had happened to us since being captured by Halok and his tribe was diminishing. Apart from our appearance, we were in good shape.

'They wouldn't dare enter Repartimento,' he said. 'And it is not much out of our way. And we could get fresh clothes,' he added as the thought struck him.

'What a good idea, José, an outfitters will be the first place to go when we arrive there. We daren't be seen anywhere else until you've replaced those,' I said, indicating his makeshift attire. 'We could celebrate our survival from all of our trials and wind down a little. We could have a night on the town and perhaps stay overnight,' I enthused further. 'The worst of our journey is over and with fresh clothes and a night in a good hotel we could look forward to Manaus in a happier frame of mind.'

José raised his hand to prevent me going overboard with my fertile imagination.

'Hold on a minute, Martin, Repartimento is much bigger than you imagine and it's much better if we keep to the outskirts that I know.'

What started as a casual remark by José now became paramount in our minds for the rest of the night.

As we enjoyed our nightcap and relived some of the events of our journey together, I saw an excitement in his eyes that I'd only seen on a few occasions. Despite his many years' experience in the rainforest and as a guide, it was doubtful if even he had ever had such an adventure.

Chapter 26

We saw the hazy smoke of Repartimento long before the buildings came into view. I could already see what he meant by the size of it. José had already explained much of the layout of the place as he'd called there on several occasions with tourists. I was once more aware of my ignorance of places unknown to me before I came here. They are huge, industrial towns and cities. I had imagined finding remote villages in this vast rainforest. As we drew closer, the myriad lights were enough to see the wisdom of José's advice to avoid the centre.

We sneaked in as it was getting dusk, to a section that José was familiar with. In the state we were in we could have been arrested on sight otherwise. Even though it was on the edge of town, the supermarket José had in mind was quite a distance from our mooring and we walked it.

It was a large supermarket, open till midnight and the security guard kept a close eye on us as we moved around. We quickly bought some clothes and I followed José to the toilets on the outside of the building. We dressed into our new outfits and left the discarded ones in a skip. We re-entered and found the large café. After eating a tasty meal that was hot in the manner of chilli, we washed it down with a cold beer. Feeling much better, we booked into a small hotel close by that José had used before. It was comfortable and cheap. We had no luggage of course, and they didn't accept credit cards, so it was cash up front. We had a shower of sorts; the water was tepid and dribbled from the head, but I felt better for it. I would have preferred better accommodation but my friend had only ever availed himself of this sort for obvious reasons. The big hotels in central Repartimento were for the rich Americans and businessmen, he said. His tourist clients used those, but he couldn't afford them.

We walked a short distance and into a bar that José had frequented before on his previous visits. I could see he knew some of the men in there and I was welcomed with the same warmth as they gave him. Of course I felt a little out of it to begin with, as they gabbled away in Portuguese. I could see he was telling them about some of our adventures and explaining who I was. They took turns in grabbing my hand, hugging me and gently slapping my face like a long lost brother. He must have explained how I had coped with the various pitfalls and I was no longer a stranger but a hero. Then it was drinks all round till the early morning. I attempted to stick to beer, but very little was available, José informed me. They all seemed to be drinking from a bottle of amber-coloured spirit. Each in turn bought a bottle of it at the bar and shared it out till it was gone. Then it was the next man's turn. We all kept our own glass, so it was a simple way of getting drunk. When it was my turn I understood why José came here. It was also the cheapest way to get drunk. Although I knew little Portuguese, at the end of the night I understood most of the sign language and rude gestures that are universal amongst male-only conversations. The nods and the winks towards a girl working behind the bar and then to José, told me another reason why he had come here on previous occasions.

Chapter 27

Repartimento disappeared from sight and the two disparate offsprings of William Henry Lockwood sat contentedly side-by-side looking forward to a relatively easy journey back to Manaus. No longer guide and tourist, they were brothers in every sense of the word, closely bonded by what they had endured together.

I looked at José out of the corner of my eye in his new outfit. I could smell the after-shave I had let him sample in the hotel bedroom before we'd left. Both of us had visited a barber's and had a haircut and our beards shaved off. His thick black hair was shining with a coating of hair cream. I got the impression that our adventures were over. He didn't want to soil his new clothes. I had spent little money since arriving in Brazil except for my escorts on the first night, so I insisted on splashing out for both our outfits in the supermarket.

After that enjoyable evening in the city, our journey to Manaus would be a bit of an anti-climax but it was all we were thinking about. I had more than enough photos to fill my needs and it was full speed ahead. Despite the fact that we were going with the current, José had the outboard at full throttle.

The next place on the way was Maravilha, but we wouldn't be stopping there. We'd bought enough food in Repartimento in the way of bread and tinned stuff to see us safely through to Manaus. We could still catch fish and gather fresh fruit on the way, but no more tramping through the forest and soiling our new clothes. We would arrive in Manaus as if we had been on a gentle sightseeing cruise. He wanted his fellow tour operators to think he'd had an easy time for his money. What really happened at the end would be our secret.

Distance and time is very vague on the rivers, but I guessed Maravilha was about fifty miles and we should reach there before nightfall. Despite our new clothes, the weather hadn't changed and the humidity was still as bad. There was no paddling upstream in water too shallow for the motor, so it was less exhausting. Apart from more different species I captured on camera, the day was uneventful. We moored in sight of Maravilha and I for one, applied numerous creams and sprays I'd purchased in Repartimento. They were guaranteed to drive off any insect in Brazil; they didn't of course, but by now I stopped looking for the bites and scratching them.

The next day we came to the *Arquipélago das Anavilhana*. We had passed through here in the reverse direction on our first journey to meet the Nucutanis. Despite our urgency, José said the vast flood plain with its many islands was worth spending extra time to explore. It was a once in a lifetime opportunity and we decided to give it some time.

Apart from the direction of the current, it would be easy to get lost, such is the vast area of water. Islands split this up and of course their shape and size change so much it could never be mapped accurately. José demonstrated his skill with the boat and we spent several hours exploring the islands. The boat went with and against the different currents and between vast islands, each one worth a visit, with wildlife that was obvious to see as we startled them; all for the benefit of my camera. It was a wonderful climax to my time in Brazil and all that was left was a leisurely return to Manaus. We think we saw the shadow of a puma at the edge of the water one day, but it disappeared before I got my camera out. We never did see a jaguar.

The next morning I woke knowing that this would be our last day on the boat, and felt a little sad. The death of the Indian guard would never go away. It was something I would find difficult not to disclose when I related my experiences after a few beers. Nobody would believe me anyway. They would probably think I had been delirious with some tropical disease.

The sun was out and a slight breeze made it one of the better days of my time here. The Rio Negro was getting wider as we approached Manaus. The noise of the howlers and macaws lessened with each mile. It was if they had been forever trying to get rid of us with their screeching, and now we were leaving there was no need to keep it up. Gradually the sound of the city replaced it. Ship sirens welcomed us, unknowingly of course. We pulled into a mooring space and I jumped off to tie up. I climbed back on to pick up my backpack expecting to find José getting his own things together. He'd remained seated on the bench and motioned me to sit beside him.

'Let us sit here for a while, Martin. I will fetch two excellent cups of coffee from a café across the road. It's something I do when I moor up after a journey. We'll rest for a while before we drive back to my flat.'

It was unexpected but as it was still early afternoon and there was no rush, I did as he said. He returned and I had two measures of brandy ready from the last of the bottle. We could toast our safe return, I said.

We touched the two cups of neat spirit and drank them down. We slowly sipped the strong coffee. I was hooked on it. Cappuccino would never fill the gap when I got back. The large brandy lulled my senses. I remembered Frank Sinatra's version of "The Coffee Song", making light of Brazil's coffee surplus, with a line about a politician's daughter being fined for drinking water as all drinks other than coffee are banned. The sun was warm through the trees and despite the noise of the city, I felt mellow. My mind was already thinking of the journey home to Cornwall, the Eden Project and other fantasies. I felt exhilarated and triumphant at the same time. It was an achievement I would never surpass. I glanced at José, intending to pass on my thoughts. My euphoria disappeared. I could see he had other things on his mind; his brow was furrowed. It was the reason for the break. What new revelation was he about to impart? I had to be patient.

It was five minutes before he began to satisfy my curiosity.

'You remember our time in the village of the Winukanatus?' He didn't wait for a reply. 'Halok woke you and I was being beaten by him. I think he would have beaten me to death because I am from another tribe, that much I could tell even though his language is different to the Nucutanis. Because you are a stranger from the outside world, you were more of a capture. You were to be sacrificed. Your head would have been a trophy. After being shrunk he would carry it around at his waist. I said the only thing that would save us. I told him that your father came many years ago into their village. I shouted it for all to hear. The elders remembered him and they argued with Halok. I had guessed the truth and thought I had won the day, knowing how my family had loved him and hoping they had loved him too. Then I realised our father was more than a welcome visitor. In the time he was with the Winukanatus he passed their extra initiation test, their highest honour, and had the blue scar on his arm that proved it. He had his pick of the maidens and then escaped before possible death. He loved my mother and wanted to return to her. It became clear to me from what the elders muttered, that Halok was the offspring and is our brother also.' It was a bombshell.

I stared at José when he said this. William Henry Lockwood, his name stood out in gold lettering on the headstone. His second name had never really registered in my mind before. He once told me that at Oxford there was another William Lockwood and so everyone called him Henry, which they shortened to Hal.

José had pointed out to Halok that he was the offspring of William Henry, hoping for mercy because we were all brothers. This obviously had had the opposite effect and he had become enraged. His father had abandoned him; now he could kill us for spite. What José said next confirmed this.

'Instead of saving our lives I had made things worse. Despite protests from the elders, we were both to be sacrificed, and have a slow death at that. Halok would wreak his revenge on the two of us.'

I had admired my father for his an adventurous spirit, and still did, but these revelations showed a different side to him. He had taken advantage of the Winukanatus' offer of the pick of the young maidens and then made his escape. He had no intentions of living with them.

My thoughts on José hadn't changed. He was the love child, fathered by trickery on the part of the Nucutanis. I think William Henry Lockwood had really loved José's mother and provided for his education and upkeep because of it.

José seemed surprised that I wasn't upset after he revealed that Halok was our brother, and the things my father had done amongst the tribes he had met. Perhaps it was the brandy or the warm day. Perhaps it was because we'd escaped from Halok's clutches. Perhaps it was finding a flaw in my dad's armour and that he had been human after all. I laughed out loud.

'Do you think our beloved father went round looking for these tribes and siring children and that there are many more young Lockwoods undiscovered José? He saw the point of my humour and that I was joking. We roared with laughter at the idea.

I stayed with José for a few days and we celebrated in style. Despite discovering he was my half-brother and the close friendship we had enjoyed, we knew there was no future for us together. We were from different worlds. Before I left, I handed him a box containing a laptop. I bought it when we went shopping in Manaus one day. He thought it was for myself. I promised to send him flash drives of all the photographs I had taken throughout. I'd edit them all first and by then he should be able to see them on his new present. We would keep in touch but that was all.

Chapter 28

I took a taxi out to Philippe Sousa's factory. He was delighted to see me and after a strong coffee in his office, he asked if he could come to my hotel that night and if we could share a meal together. I'd told him how successful it had been as far as the photographs I had taken. He put the cards in his office computer and I had a preview at the same time. I'd only seen them on the camera's small screen before that. Some serious editing needed to be done but I was satisfied the camera had done its job and I had more than enough good pictures. He even downloaded them into his hard drive, to show his friends he said. Such was his admiration of them.

'I will show my friends the difference between these and what they have only seen at the INPA,' he laughed. I could see he was genuinely impressed.

True to his word, he arrived at the hotel that evening and we enjoyed a meal of his choosing that was excellent. He insisted on paying. We retired to the bar afterwards. I described the journey as any tourist would, enlarging on the wonders of the flora and fauna. I left it at that. I thanked him for putting me in touch with José in the beginning.

'He must be the best guide in Manaus, and I would certainly recommend him.' It was said very much tongue in cheek.

He was so pleased the trip had turned out well, he said. 'Trip' was an understatement of course, but I didn't enlighten him with details of all the traumas, pitfalls and discoveries I'd made regarding José and Halok. I'd an idea he would find out anyway eventually from José's uncle. The twinkle in his dark eyes as he listened, hinted that he already knew.

It was only then that the penny dropped. As soon as he knew my name on that first meeting, he already knew about my father and José's relationship from Jose's uncle. It was why he put me in touch with him. He had steered me into safe hands. I think the enlightenment in my expression was noticeable. I gripped his hand firmly and gave a wry smile. There was no need for me to spell it out.

'Thank you,' I said. 'I can see why you are a successful businessman.'

'I too, am glad we met by chance in the hotel when you arrived,' he replied. 'You look much wiser than when I first saw you, and I must admit I feared for your safety and survival. It is good that you give so much credit to José for retracing your father's footsteps. I shall tell his uncle so, he will be pleased.'

Chapter 29

It was over a year before a vacancy became available at the Eden Project. I was in no hurry. It was where I wanted to be. When I entered the dome containing the South American microclimate for the first time again, I visualised José's dark features with his beard and the cigar clenched between his teeth. It was not as hot and steamy of course; the visitors wouldn't be able to stand it. It's certainly not as dangerous as the real thing, but I enjoy the memories as I work there. Visitors ask me about the various plants and I'm happy to tell them to the best of my ability. Sometimes my mind wings its way back to the rainforest and I'm transported back in time. José is pointing out the plant in its natural environment and my tongue runs away with me. They seem surprised at the intensity and detail of my answers.